"I'm not a chef, darlin', but I'd say you've been cooked."

Dylan smiled. A gentleman would probably retrieve the towel draped on a lounge chair near the hot tub, then turn his back as she slipped it around herself. But both options seemed kind of dull to him. He raised his eyebrows. *Dare you.*

He faked a yawn. "This is real comfortable. Of course, if you were to offer me a room, that would probably be even more comfy. You said you had just one guest at the moment. Which means you've got a few rooms available. Why not put me up?"

"Bastard," she muttered. Then, even as he was congratulating himself on a hand well played, she added, "I've had enough."

She stood, and took her time getting out of the hot tub and replacing the lid. Her body gleamed. Taut muscles, curved lines, gorgeous legs. She turned from him to reach for her towel. Methodically, she patted off the moisture beaded on her skin—then tossed the towel on the chair again.

"Good night," she said, her hand on the patio door.

So she was really going to leave him out there, with no transportation back to town.

"About tonight…"

"Yeah?" His confidence surged. After all, she'd once loved him. He'd once been her best friend.

"There's an extra stall in the barn," she said. "If you're desperate, you can have that."

Dear Reader,

Have you noticed that the most wonderful, magical days come about, not as a result of careful planning and organization, but almost by accident? *Serendipity* is one of my favorite words. And the perfect example occurred several years ago when my husband and I and my two daughters, along with my husband's father and his wife, were driving out to Kananaskis to enjoy "Mozart of the Mountain."

A bad traffic jam had us aborting our plans and heading instead for the small mountain town of Canmore. Within half an hour of turning off the highway, we were in a large yellow raft, drifting along Alberta's Bow River. The day was warm and bright, we still had our picnic and the scenery, dominated by the Three Sisters Mountain, amazed us all. At the end of that perfect, unplanned day we were left with a memory to treasure forever.

And I had the setting for a trilogy I'd been thinking about. The Shannon sisters have always counted on one another, especially since, like their mother, they seem to be unlucky in love. Three men are set to change all that, with three proposals as unique as the sisters who inspire them. I hope you enjoy A *Second-Chance* Proposal, A *Convenient* Proposal and A *Lasting* Proposal.

Sincerely,

C.J. *Carmichael*

P.S. I'd love to hear from you. Please send mail to the following Canadian address: #1754—246 Stewart Green S.W., Calgary, Alberta T3H 3C8, Canada. Or send e-mail to: cjcarmichael@home.com

A Second-Chance Proposal
C.J. Carmichael

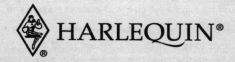

HARLEQUIN®

TORONTO • NEW YORK • LONDON
AMSTERDAM • PARIS • SYDNEY • HAMBURG
STOCKHOLM • ATHENS • TOKYO • MILAN • MADRID
PRAGUE • WARSAW • BUDAPEST • AUCKLAND

ISBN 0-373-71038-0

A SECOND-CHANCE PROPOSAL

This edition published by arrangement with Harlequin Books S.A.

® and TM are trademarks of the publisher. Trademarks indicated with
® are registered in the United States Patent and Trademark Office, the
Canadian Trade Marks Office and in other countries.

Visit us at www.eHarlequin.com

Printed in U.S.A.

ACKNOWLEDGMENTS

Thanks to those who assisted me in my research,
in particular Corporal Patrick Webb of the RCMP in Calgary,
Constable Barry Beales of the RCMP Canmore Detachment
and Lynn Martel, a reporter with the *Canmore Leader*.

DEDICATION

This trilogy is dedicated to my editors,
Beverley Sotolov and Paula Eykelhof,
with my thanks and affection.

CHAPTER ONE

CHILLED CURRENTS of mountain air circled the Larch Lodge bed-and-breakfast and played on Cathleen Shannon's bare wet shoulders. The cold autumn air only made the luxury of 104-degree bubbling water all the more pleasurable. Fitting her body to the sloped back of the hot tub's molded seat, she gazed upward. A sky of restless clouds offered teasing glimpses of a fluorescent half-moon.

This is nice. She took a sip of brandy from the plastic glass she'd brought out with her. The outdoor spa had been installed this summer for the benefit of her guests, but she really should make use of it more often herself.

She sighed and sank lower, then suddenly tensed as a shadow shifted in the dark, about twenty meters away. Something, or someone, was out there. But why wasn't Kip barking? The shape kept moving, coming closer. Oh, why had she turned off all the house lights?

Probably she was worried about nothing. Elk roamed freely over her property. Still, there was the off chance it could be a bear.... She contemplated dashing for the house, but just then, against the backdrop of moonlight, she made out the silhouette of a lanky cowboy. She recognized him immediately from the set of his shoulders and the rhythm of his gait.

Unbelievable.

And there, trotting faithfully by his boots, was *her* dog. The traitor.

Like a figure in a dream, the cowboy kept advancing. She couldn't see his eyes—clouds had shifted yet again to cover the moon—but she had no doubt that he watched her every step of the way. Only when he reached the cedar skirting around the tub did he stop.

"Well, well," she said coolly, hiding her trembling hands under the water. According to his cousin, Jake Hartman, Dylan was supposed to be in Reno, Nevada, the latest stop in his never-ending rodeo circuit. Jake always filled her in on Dylan's latest adventures, even though she'd let him know she couldn't care less what her ex-fiancé was up to. Still, when Jake talked, she rarely missed a single word. And she was certain that plans of Dylan McLean's return to Canmore had never been mentioned.

If they had, she would've prepared herself. Over the past two years she'd come up with at least a dozen speeches with which to rake him over the coals. Trouble was, now that he stood just a few feet away, she couldn't think of a single word, let alone a whole tirade.

He closed in on her, then sat on the decking, folding his arms over the tub's white plastic ledge. Now she could see his face clearly. His gray eyes sought to engage hers, to coax a smile, but she was in no mood to be charmed. Eventually his gaze skimmed from her face, down her neck, to the line where the water cut across the top of her chest.

"I like your outfit," he said. "Room in there for one more?"

After two years of silence, you'd think he'd have managed to come up with something a little more profound.

"The hot tub is for lodge guests only. Oh, and family and *friends*."

He registered the intended insult with a one-sided twist of his mouth. "I see. And I'm neither. Is that it?"

She said nothing.

"Look, Cathleen." He sighed and tipped back his hat a fraction. "Things ended badly between us, but you know it wasn't what I wanted. If I'd had a choice..." He reached for her shoulder, and she pulled away instinctively.

"Hell, Cathleen. I wasn't going to hurt you."

"Don't touch me."

"Okay." Dylan shifted back on his heels. "You've got a right to be angry. But you received the letter, right? Jake said he put it directly in your hands.''

''Yeah, Dylan. Thanks a lot for going to the trouble.''

She pictured herself two years ago, standing at the open screen door of this very house, staring off into space. Her white dress flowed down to her sandaled feet. Her long, normally rather wild dark hair coiled in luxurious curls down her back. Two bouquets of orchids—one larger than the other—lay at the ready on the kitchen table.

She held an envelope in her hand. With her name on the front, penned in Dylan's distinctive bold script. Out in the distance, the dust from Jake's truck still hovered like a patch of white fog in the lane.

She hadn't needed to tear open the flap and read the single sheet of paper within to know there would be no wedding that day.

''I guess you didn't think your note ought to be supplemented by something as personal as a visit or a phone call.''

He winced. ''I was afraid you might talk me out of my decision. But you've got to admit the situation was impossible. There was no way we could've gotten married as we'd planned.''

She'd admit nothing of the kind. But she didn't argue with him. If he'd cared what she thought, he would have talked this over with her two years ago.

"I'm sorry you had to deal with the aftermath—telling the guests, canceling the minister and the caterer…"

Actually, her sisters had handled those details for her, but she didn't want to give him the comfort of knowing that. Besides, the logistics of the wedding arrangements had been the least of her heartaches back then. She held out her arms, skimming the bubbles that frothed on the water's surface. It still bothered her how much his desertion had hurt. She saw it as a sign of weakness in herself, and weakness was something she could not tolerate.

"What did you do with the ring?" Dylan was staring at her hands, naked of jewelry of any type.

"I sold it," she told him, improvising. "Just like I sold the wedding dress. Advertising them both in the *Canmore Leader*. I used the money to finance the renovations to this place."

"Yeah, Jake told me you opened in the spring of last year. He says—" Dylan leaned back and stretched out his legs "—Jake says you've dated a little."

"A little," she agreed amicably. Actually, the tally was close to a dozen men in two years. An active social life had seemed the best way to prove to the town, her sisters and even herself that her botched wedding hadn't been such a big deal.

Dylan rubbed his chin. "So who's the current favorite?"

She hated the fact that he made them sound like jelly-bean flavors. "Actually, I've been seeing two guys lately. Friday, Thad Springer and I went to a movie in Banff."

"Springer? You mean RCMP *Staff Sergeant* Springer?"

"I sure do."

"Jesus, Cathleen…" He took a second to digest that, before asking, "And the other?"

"James Strongman."

If she'd surprised him with Thad, she shocked him with James.

"I don't believe this. You're kidding me, right?"

"I assure you, I'm totally serious."

"Of all the men in Canmore…you *wouldn't* date my stepbrother…."

"Why is that, Dylan? Because you never got along with the man? Because you hate his father? Those are *your* issues, not mine." Although she *had* put off James for more than a year simply because of his ties to Dylan. But James had been persistent. And still was. On their last date he'd made it clear he hoped for a more exclusive relationship with her.

"You'll think I'm just being jealous, but you should stay away from that man. You can't trust him."

"You mean if he asked me to marry him—which

I think he just might do—he'd back out the day of the ceremony?''

"You know I had no choice...."

Liar! He'd had a choice. And he'd made it without even considering that she might have an opinion on the matter.

"Just for the record," he volunteered, "there's been no one in my life—*no one*—since you."

Ah. She turned her head and blinked. For a moment she wondered if he was telling the truth, then she reminded herself that it simply didn't matter.

"I don't know why you think I'd be interested in the sorry state of your love life. Dylan, this whole conversation is pointless. Why don't you just go back to wherever you came from?"

"I can't. Jake gave me a ride and now he's gone."

She hadn't heard a thing over the sound of the hot-tub motor and jets. "Well, that was a really stupid thing to do."

"I kind of specialize in really stupid things."

Even if that was genuine regret on his face, it couldn't make any difference. Being sorry didn't change a damn thing.

"Oh hell, Dylan. What're you *really* doing here?"

He removed his cowboy hat. "I was back in Canmore. How could I not come to see you? Like you said, I owed you an apology. In person."

''So you're looking for forgiveness. Is that it?''

''Now that you mention it, do you think you ever could?''

''Dylan, I consider myself lucky that our wedding never took place. If that's forgiveness enough for you, then you're welcome to it. So why don't you let yourself into the kitchen and phone Jake to come and pick you up.''

Dylan frowned, then slipped a pack she hadn't noticed off his shoulders. He set the canvas bag on the deck and balanced his hat casually on top of it. ''I can't call Jake. He's on his way to Calgary. Flies out tomorrow morning for a three-week tour of Australia while his town house is being remodeled. Paint, carpets, the works. I'd stay there, but the furniture's in storage, and the fumes are something awful.''

Wasn't that convenient timing? But his story was probably true. She'd known for some time that Jake had planned a trip for this summer. And on the last occasion she'd run into him, he'd been standing in front of the display of paint chips at the local hardware store, contemplating the subtle difference in tone between ''tumbleweed'' and ''flax.''

''In case you've forgotten, Canmore is a tourist town. There are plenty of motels and other bed-and-breakfasts.''

''Yeah, but somehow none of them seemed to have a room available once I gave them my name.''

So the old rumors hadn't died. It was all such nonsense she couldn't believe it.

"And this is my problem because...?" She reached for the controls to the hot-tub jets, but was stymied when Dylan laid his hand over hers. She hated how familiar his touch was, right down to the rough cowboy calluses. This time it took her several seconds before she jerked away.

"I told you—"

"Oh, yeah. No touching. I'm sorry, but it's hard. You're still so beautiful. Even more than I remembered."

She resented the compliment as much as his touch. Whatever was going on just didn't add up...

Then suddenly she understood. He wasn't really here to apologize. He'd come expecting he could turn on the old charm and she'd crumple at his feet. He'd end up with a place to stay *and* a woman in his bed.

"Well, I wish I could say the same for you," she said. "What happened to your forehead? And your shoulder?" The scar was new, one she'd noticed when he raked back his thick dark hair with his hands. As for his shoulder, he held it stiffly when he walked.

Dylan acknowledged his injuries with a shrug.

"You idiot. Do you think you could've found a more dangerous rodeo event than bull riding?"

"Hey, I wore off a lot of anger on those babies.

And won a good pile of money at the same time. Figured I could pay down the rest of your mortgage.''

She refused to see anything sweet or honorable in the offer. ''So now you're trying to buy me off. As if I would touch your money.''

He'd put up most of the down payment on the house, which they'd registered in her name for legal and tax reasons. In his note, he'd told her to keep it, sell it, whatever she wanted. Covering the mortgage payments while financing the renovations had been a struggle, but selling the house hadn't been an option she could bear. Even though she would have loved to throw his portion of the down payment in his face. Of course, his face hadn't been around for her to throw *anything* at.

''I don't need your money, Dylan. This place pays for itself.''

''I heard you've been busy. Anyone staying with you right now?''

''Just one guest at the moment.'' But once the snow fell and skiing season started, she'd be full again, as she had been all summer.

Dylan put a hand on his pack. ''Which means you've got a few rooms available.''

She should have seen that one coming. Folding her arms over her chest, she narrowed her eyes at him. ''The answer is *no*.''

''Cathleen, you're hurting my feelings.''

"We've already established your feelings don't run much deeper than the bark on a birch tree."

He adjusted the position of his hat, balancing it carefully on the top of the canvas pack. "Well, you're probably right about that. Fortunately, yours don't, either. Got rid of the dress and the ring—wasn't that what you said?"

"Damn right."

"Well, then. Why not put me up? I'll pay for one month up front."

"A month!"

"At least. I've got a little unfinished business here in Canmore."

"Like what?"

"Family business. Old scores to settle."

"What are you talking about?"

He propped an elbow against the hot-tub edge and made himself comfortable. "You know as well as I do. I haven't been able to forget about that poor kid."

Jilly Beckett. The memory of the teenager shot down in cold blood on the McLean ranch made Cathleen shiver, despite the heated water surrounding her. "The family had a memorial for her a year after it happened, Dylan. I went. For a sixteen-year-old, she was pretty accomplished."

"She would've turned eighteen this year. She'd be starting university...."

"They never did arrest anyone." There simply

wasn't enough evidence. Not that lack of proof had stopped people from drawing their own conclusions.

"Cathleen, did you ever think I—"

She shook her head. Like so many things, it was too late for him to ask that question.

Pain pinched his features. "For the record, I didn't."

"Don't you think I know that? God, Dylan, you're so dense sometimes."

He turned his head, facing out into the dark. "Ain't that the truth."

Above their heads a cloud drifted by and the moon washed the deck in light. Dylan faced her again. "If I'm innocent, that means the real killer is out there. And you know what's really scary?"

She was almost afraid to ask. "What?"

"He's living with my mother."

"YOU THINK your stepfather shot Jilly Beckett?" Cathleen asked.

"I do." He glanced at her, then forced his gaze back out into the night. It was impossible to forget, for even one minute, that she was naked in the hot tub. Not that he could see much—beyond the dark outline of her breasts. But just knowing was enough.

He'd come here with the faintest of hopes and almost no expectations, never guessing the gods would choose to mock him in this way. He had a need, like a deep thirst, to drink in the sight of her. Still, he'd noticed she got restless and uncomfortable if he looked at her for too long.

"When did you arrive at this conclusion?"

"It took me longer than it should've," he admitted. "I was too busy feeling sorry for myself." That he'd lost the love of his life. That he'd probably be an old man before he was finally able to ranch his own land again. That his own mother thought he was a vicious murderer...

But last month he'd been hospitalized—first serious injury since he'd started rodeo life—and the downtime had given him plenty of opportunity for reflection.

"Assuming you're right, what can you do about it?"

"I don't know. But my mother is living with this creep. I've got to come up with something." A conclusion confirmed by his recent conversation with Jake. He wondered if Cathleen had the same concerns. "Have you seen Rose lately?"

"No. After our wedding was canceled, dropping in for coffee seemed inappropriate. How about you? Have you kept in touch?"

He heard the recrimination in her voice, as if she expected the answer to be no. But he'd tried. "Mom didn't answer any of my letters or accept my calls." He rubbed a dirty spot on the knee of his jeans and wondered if he dared ask. What the hell, she could only say no.

"I plan on dropping in on her tomorrow. I don't expect she'll be thrilled to see me, but if you were there, too, she probably wouldn't slam the door in my face."

Cathleen had always been a favorite of his mother's. When they'd announced their engagement, Rose had said she was glad because she'd thought of Cathleen as a daughter for many years already.

"I heard she was ill and not accepting visitors at all."

"Yeah. Jake said as much, too." And he didn't know what to make of it. His mother had always been a little shy, but she'd been friendly and hospitable once she got to know a person.

"Chances are that even if we drop by, she won't let us in."

"Maybe. Maybe not."

She examined his face, then nodded. "I suppose it's worth a try. It would be good for her to see you."

He stirred the chlorinated water with one hand. "You know Mom isn't the only reason I came back to Canmore."

"You're talking about your ranch, I suppose."

Actually, he'd been talking about her.

"Lots has changed at the Thunder Bar M," she

told him. "The ranch isn't even being operated anymore. Your mom and Max have moved into town."

"Yeah—Jake told me. He said Max hired some kind of caretaker to look after the place. Do you know who it is?"

"Danny Mizzoni. He's living in the main house, with his wife and two kids."

Dylan swore. "That drug-head?" The man had been convicted of selling narcotics to thirteen-year-olds at the local junior high. "Wasn't he in jail when I left town?"

"Danny was paroled a year after we were engaged. And Max was reelected mayor of Canmore, on a pro-development platform."

Canmore, just fifteen minutes from Banff National Park, had always been a battleground between those who wanted to capitalize on the town's proximity to the famous park and those concerned about preserving the natural beauty and wildlife habitat of the surrounding area.

"Pro-development. Well, that figures." Lots had changed, all right, and it made him tired. Mentally, as well as physically. A good night's sleep was what he needed. Trouble was, he didn't have a bed for the night. Not yet, anyway.

He noticed how flushed Cathleen's face was getting. As she allowed her feet to float up and out of the water, he could see that even her toes had turned red.

"I'm not a chef, darlin', but I'd say you've been cooked."

"I *usually* limit myself to twenty minutes. You've kept me in here almost double that, I'd guess. Why don't you go into the kitchen for a drink. I'll join you in a minute."

He smiled. A gentleman would probably do just as she'd asked, or, at a minimum, retrieve the towel draped on a nearby lounge chair, then turn his back as she slipped it around herself.

But both options seemed kind of dull to him. He glanced from the towel back to her, then raised his eyebrows. Without a word spoken, it was out there. *Dare you.*

She glared at him.

He faked a yawn. "This is real comfortable. I could sit here all night."

"Oh, really?"

"Of course, if you were to offer me a room, that would probably be even more comfy."

"Bastard," she muttered. Then, even as he was congratulating himself on a hand well played, she added, "I've had enough."

She stood, and took her time climbing out of the tub and replacing the lid.

Her body gleamed. Taut muscles, curved lines, gorgeous legs. In the moonlight her skin was honey-brown—except for the creamy places protected from the summer sun by her bikini.

She turned away from him to reach for her towel. Methodically she patted off the moisture beaded on her skin—then tossed the towel back onto the chair.

Completely naked, completely beautiful, she strolled to the patio doors, then turned back casually. The coldness in her eyes slapped down his libido as effectively as a pail of cold water over the head.

She hated him. Almost immediately he rejected the impression. She was still angry, that was all. She'd get over it.

"Good night," she said, her hand on the patio door.

So she was really going to do it. Leave him out here, with no method of transportation back to town. He schooled himself for the added insult of having the door locked in his face.

"About tonight..." she said.

"Yeah?" His confidence surged. After all, once she'd loved him. Once he'd been her best friend.

"There's an extra stall in the barn," she said. "If you're desperate, you can have that."

CHAPTER TWO

CATHLEEN SAT IN THE DARK of her office for several minutes. She had no idea what Dylan would do. Would he walk the eight kilometers back to Canmore? Start banging on her door, demanding a room? Or actually settle down in the barn, as she'd invited him to?

When she heard the sound of water rushing through pipes to the outside tap, she retrieved her towel from the deck, then cautiously made her way through the darkened hallway to the dining room. Through a clump of overgrown lilac bushes, the barn light glowed. Unless Cascade, the horse Dylan had given her as a wedding present, had developed an opposable thumb, he'd decided to take her up on her incredibly generous offer.

In her situation, most women would've kicked the bum out, she was certain. Which just showed what a tolerant, kindhearted soul she was.

Upstairs she showered and changed into a nightgown. After brushing her teeth, she was still too wound up for sleep. She needed to talk, which meant calling one of her sisters. Maureen, the eldest, had to get up early to work at her law firm in Calgary. But Kelly was on nights this week. Cathleen went back to the office and dialed the number for the local RCMP detachment.

She caught her youngest sister at her desk. "You won't believe what just happened. Dylan's back. He came by about an hour ago."

"To the B and B?" Kelly sounded indignant. Then she turned suspicious. "He didn't have the nerve to ask for a room, did he?" After a second of silence she added, "You didn't let him have one, did you?"

"Not really. I did tell him he could sleep in the stall next to Cascade, though."

Kelly laughed. "No way."

"Why not?" From the gleam in his eyes as he'd watched her get out of that hot tub, he'd been in the mood for a roll in the hay. So let him have it.

"Only you would make an offer like that. Not that it isn't better than what he deserves. What's the going rate for one of those stalls?"

"For Dylan? It'll be very steep, trust me." She propped her bare feet on top of the gray metal filing cabinet next to her desk and slid down in her chair to get comfortable.

Even more than her bedroom, this study was her place. With a desk and bookshelves at one corner, and a sofa facing a fireplace in the center of the room, it made for a cozy retreat when the B and B teemed with guests.

"Truthfully, just knowing he's out there makes me nervous," Kelly said.

"I don't know why."

"That man broke your heart."

Cathleen let her feet drop to the floor. "He did not!"

"Right." Kelly sighed. "You agreed to marry him, but never cared that much."

"I cared." It was the most she was prepared to admit. "But Dylan showed his true colors the day he walked out on me. I'm just lucky I found out in time."

Unlike her mother, who'd married their father *and* had three kids with him before she'd finally faced the truth.

"There are other reasons to be cautious...."

"Kelly, you know Dylan didn't kill that girl."

"Not on purpose—"

"Or any other way."

"Cathleen, the demonstration was getting out of hand. Tempers were hot. There was probably some pushing and shoving between the oilmen and the environmentalists. The gun could have gone off accidentally...."

"No." Regardless of their personal differences—which were mammoth—Cathleen knew Dylan was innocent on this score.

"You sound very confident."

"Why wouldn't I be? *Anyone* could've shot Jilly. You told me so yourself."

"That's true, but a number of factors weigh in against Dylan. Everyone knows he hates his stepfather so much he'd have done almost anything to stop him from drilling those wells. And running out of town the way he did sure doesn't make him appear innocent."

"Running away was stupid." *And how!* "But it isn't a crime." Not against the law, anyway.

"No. But it made him look guilty. And it doesn't help that he had an argument with his mother the night before he left. Did you know Rose sported a black eye the next day? I confess I used to like Dylan. But what kind of man hits his own mother?"

Cathleen hadn't heard this story before. Probably everyone had thought they were protecting her. Which was ridiculous, because there was no way it was true. "Dylan would never hurt his mother."

Her sister's sigh made it clear she was losing patience. "Maybe, maybe not. The point is—"

"Kel, he couldn't even find a room in town. It's almost like there's a conspiracy out there."

Kelly took a moment to answer. "I'd think you'd be glad. This isn't just about Jilly. People around here don't like what he did to you, either."

Oh, Lord. This was crazy. Yes, Dylan had been

a jerk. But she didn't want him ostracized for life. If people around town needed her to forgive him— which she wasn't ever going to do, but she *could* pretend—before they could do the same, then so be it.

"I guess I'll have to let him stay here, then."

"Cathleen, that's crazy, even for you. We've lived in Canmore all our lives, and God knows, the people here love you, always have. But if you let Dylan stay at your B and B, they'll assume you're trying to protect him. And Jilly Beckett was just sixteen years old...."

"It's nobody's business who stays at my place. And I'm the first to acknowledge that Jilly's death was a tragedy, but Dylan wasn't responsible."

"Let's say you're right about that. What about the fact that you two were once in love? Won't it be painful to have him around?"

"Don't worry, Kelly. I'm over him. Why won't anyone believe me when I tell them that?" Since when had her love life become a matter of town policy, anyway? It was bad enough that her sisters couldn't seem to butt out of her business.

After the conversation ended, Cathleen went to the cabinet by the patio doors and poured herself a brandy. She was confused about a lot of things right now, but there were two points on which she had no doubt.

Dylan hadn't killed Jilly. She would back him on

this against all of them—the townspeople, the cops, her sisters...hell, even his own mother.

Their personal relationship, however, was a different matter. If he thought he could flirt and tease his way back into her heart, he'd soon discover he was wrong. His apology tonight hadn't cut it by half. That man had walked out on her.

And she was going to make him pay.

DYLAN AWOKE COLD, STIFF and bad tempered. Through narrowed eyes he spied his roommate, a sturdy little quarter horse with a spotted coat. At the same moment, she turned her head to the side and focused one dark-lashed brown eye at him.

"Sleep well?" he asked, propping his back against the wooden wall. Pain stabbed through his left shoulder, and he brought up his right hand protectively. In her stall, Cascade snorted.

"Me, neither." This wasn't his first time crashing out on a stable floor, but he was definitely getting too old for this—

Plop, plop. Cascade didn't even blink as she performed her morning purge.

Dylan wrinkled his nose. He'd worked with the smell of horses all his life. But usually he'd had his first coffee of the day before he did so.

He pulled himself upright, then gave Cascade a pat on her flank. "We'll talk more later," he promised. He brushed the straw from his jeans and put on a clean shirt from his backpack. Carrying both his hat and his shaving kit, he tugged open the barn door, then strained to close it behind him.

Outside he paused, pulling in lungfuls of the crisp mountain air and scanning the landscape. Cathleen's property sat on the northern edge of Thunder Valley, tucked in a vee, with the Three Sisters Mountain to the southeast and Mount Lawrence Grassi to the southwest. North lay the Bow River, then the Trans-Canada Highway, which linked Canmore to the bustling city of Calgary, one hour east.

When the property had come on the market more than two years ago, Cathleen had immediately been taken by the possibilities of the house. He'd loved the land it sat on and that it was adjacent to the Thunder Bar M. He'd hoped to one day combine the two properties. But that was a distant dream now.

He rubbed his chin, then headed for the house. Looking up, he wondered which bedroom window belonged to Cathleen. God, the sight of her getting out of that hot tub last night was something he'd never forget. Trust her to have the nerve. They'd pulled some crazy stunts together when they were younger, and Cathleen had never been able to resist a dare. So that much hadn't changed.

But, as she'd pointed out last night, lots else had. Maybe he should've hiked back to Canmore and tried to find someplace else to stay. He had to admit their reunion scene hadn't gone as well as it could have. He'd kind of hoped she would yell at him and throw a few dishes around the place, then let him pull her into his arms and make it all up to her. But she'd been worse than angry. She'd been cold and aloof. How was he supposed to deal with *that?*

He stopped at the outdoor tap to brush his teeth and shave—a pain at the best of times, miserable when all you had was cold water. This day wasn't off to the best of starts. He didn't like his odds at being offered breakfast, but he'd settle for a good, hot cup of coffee. Hat in hand, he stepped up the painted boards of the porch steps—she'd replaced the former rotting structure—then knocked at the screen.

The wafting scents were tantalizing. Eggs and coffee and something baking.

He tapped on the wooden frame again. "Can I come in?"

"Sure." An elderly woman flipped the latch on the screen door. Her impossibly red curls were tied back with a turquoise scarf that matched her belted pantsuit. She had on bright red lipstick and a generous dash of perfume. "Cathleen said you'd be up any minute. You're that man who ran out on her the morning of your wedding, aren't you? Cathleen told me the story."

He ran a hand over his face, expecting recriminations. None came.

"Sit down, son. I'll make you some breakfast."

Dylan scratched the top of his head, slightly bewildered. Why was this woman offering to cook him breakfast? And where was Cathleen?

He sat, though, after tucking his denim shirt into his jeans. It seemed wiser to go with the flow for the moment. No sooner was his butt in a chair than a mug of steaming coffee was set in front of him, along with a muffin and a sectioned grapefruit. He appreciated the coffee. Wasn't so sure about the muffin. After giving it a prod, he tore off a smidgen and slipped it to Kip. The dog gobbled it as if it were a prime cut of steak.

"Um, thanks. Is Cathleen…?"

"She's outside doing something with the hot tub. Checking pH levels and adding chlorine, I think. She'll be right in. Now, how do you like your eggs?"

"Eggs?"

"Breakfast is—"

"The most important meal of the day."

Sunshine suddenly blazed through the doorway as Cathleen sailed into the room. Just the pleasure of seeing the smile she blasted in his direction was reward enough for this bizarre homecoming of his. For a moment he let himself pretend that the past two years had been a dream. That they were married and that she was smiling because she loved him and was happy to see him.

Cathleen straddled the chair opposite his and rested her chin in her hand. "You two have met each other?"

Dylan glanced at the woman by the stove. "Sure have."

"Good. Thanks, Poppy," she added as the woman placed a muffin, grapefruit and coffee in front of Cathleen.

Dylan found the whole scene confusing. Cathleen seemed perfectly content to be waited on by her elderly paying guest. "I've never heard of a bed-and-breakfast where the guests served the owners," he commented.

Cathleen held out her hands in a gesture of help-lessness. "She wakes up before I do, gets behind the stove and then won't budge."

"I'm a born cook," Poppy declared, dropping a pat of butter into a warmed frying pan. "And I need to test my recipes on someone. Besides, I've lived on my own for so long it's wonderful to have people to cook for again."

"No family?" Dylan asked.

Poppy's inner glow dimmed. "Not anymore.... Now then," she said briskly. "Something tells me you're a sunny-side-up man." She raised an egg over the frying pan. "Am I right?"

Generally he was a three-cups-of-coffee-and-nothing-else man, but he had to admit all this food smelled pretty damn good. Besides, a good breakfast might help compensate for his sleepless night. Between agonizing over the things he had said—all of them stupid and wrong—and imagining Cathleen alone in her bed, no wonder he hadn't been able to drop off.

He eyed her in her casual riding gear—jeans and boots and a Western-style shirt—and couldn't help mentally stripping her down to the outfit she'd worn last night.

She kicked him under the table just above his knee. He choked back a surprised grunt. The damn woman always had been able to read his mind too easily.

"I phoned Kelly last night," she said.

The sister who worked for the RCMP. He didn't have to think too hard to figure out what they'd been talking about. "So what did Kelly have to say about the investigation?" he asked.

"Doesn't sound like there have been any new developments in quite some time."

Cathleen sipped coffee, and he stared openly. She didn't share Kelly's perfect bone structure, or have especially pretty features like Maureen. Still, of the three sisters, she was the one who stood out in a crowd. Was it the model's wide smile, her confident dark blue eyes, those long, luscious legs...?

"What's this about?" Poppy asked, jarring him

back into the here and now as she slid two perfectly cooked eggs onto a plate, along with slices of toasted multigrain bread.

After a few moments of silence Dylan realized that Cathleen was waiting for him to answer Poppy's question.

''A couple of years ago there was a showdown on my family's ranch. My stepfather was having some petroleum company executives over for a barbecue. I'd organized a group of environmentalists for a peaceful demonstration. But events got out of hand. People started yelling and shoving. Then someone lit off a firecracker. It exploded with a burst of light and noise, of course, and the next thing we knew, the daughter of one of the oilmen, Jilly Beckett, had collapsed into her father's arms. She'd been shot.''

The sixteen-year-old's stricken face burned against his eyes, as if branded there. He hadn't pulled the trigger, but he felt his share of responsibility for leading the protest. Not that he'd had any idea a kid was going to be present.

The person he'd wanted to hurt—though not in a physical sense—had been his stepfather. The bastard had decided to allow several oil wells to be drilled on McLean property; or more precisely, he'd persuaded his wife that she should sign away her mineral rights for this purpose.

Dylan still cursed the day of their wedding. His

mother had asked him to participate in the ceremony, but he never would have cooperated if he could've guessed the changes Max Strongman and his son, James, would bring to his life.

Even now his throat thickened with the resentments that had piled up over the years, the worst from those few weeks before his scheduled wedding to Cathleen. Was he wrong to blame Rose for allowing her new husband so much control over land that had belonged to her first husband, Dylan's father? Dylan had been raised to consider the ranch his birthright, his and his cousin Jake's. But Max had other ideas.

Oil, and the money he would earn through royalties, had been Strongman's priority. Dylan could believe it, too, after years of watching his stepfather try to operate the three-thousand-acre ranch. Max had no appreciation for the beauty of the land and no respect for the creatures—either human or animal—who tried to live off it.

"The police never found the gun," Cathleen said into the quiet. "And no one on the scene saw who shot Jilly."

"Whether it was planned or not, the firecracker made an effective decoy," Dylan added.

Poppy paused in between bites of bran muffin. A tangible change had come over her while she'd processed the information. The new wariness in her eyes was one Dylan understood all too well. Being a suspect in a murder case didn't put him high on anyone's popularity list.

Cathleen seemed to have picked up on Poppy's altered mood, too. Typically, she addressed the situation head-on. "Some people assumed Dylan was guilty because he'd organized the demonstration. Plus, his differences with his stepfather were no secret. But no one ever found any evidence."

She faced Dylan. "And since nothing new has turned up in the past two years, Kelly says she doubts anyone will ever be arrested."

The look Cathleen was giving him now was almost sympathetic. "Even if Max *is* guilty, what can you possibly do about it?"

"I have no idea. But I've got to help my mother somehow." He finished off the coffee and gave her a smile that he hoped belied the insecurities that kept him awake at night. "And I've got to clear my own reputation, as well. Cathleen, darlin', I don't expect you to marry a man with a sullied reputation."

Poppy's eyebrows angled upward with alarm. "Marry?"

"Oh, just ignore him." Cathleen pushed her empty plate away. "He knows there's no way in hell I'd be stupid enough to give him a second chance."

Poppy snapped the dishrag, then folded it over the sink. "I'm going to my room to work on my cookbook for a while. Mind if I do up a vegetable pie for lunch, Cathleen? I need to make sure I've got the seasonings right...."

"Be my guest."

Which, of course, she was. Damned strangest arrangement Dylan had ever seen. Not that his arrangement with the lady of the house was much better.

Getting up from the table, he prepared to load his own dishes into the dishwasher. Cathleen made no move to stop him. This was definitely a self-serve establishment.

"Any chance we could go visit my mother later this morning? Afraid I don't have a vehicle, so we'll have to use your Jeep. I sold my truck in Reno before I caught the plane to Calgary."

"I suppose. But I have work to do, too. Don't expect me to be your personal chauffeur for the duration of your stay."

"I won't." *Duration of your stay?* Obviously, she was weakening. Now was the time to strike. "About this arrangement in the barn. I think you should know I kept Cascade awake with my snoring last night."

Cathleen's smile had a most unattractive edge of self-satisfaction to it. "Really?"

"I was wondering if I could bargain my way up to a box spring and mattress?"

She shrugged. "A few postdated checks ought to

do the trick. I've got a queen-size bed available, in the southeast-facing room.''

''Great.'' He'd get a mountain view, to boot. He had no idea why she'd changed her mind about his staying, but it was an encouraging first step. Right after the dishes, he'd make out a check, for whatever sum she demanded. Then he'd have to start working on a new strategy. One that would see him moving from the guest bed into *hers*.

It was a nice thought, if a trifle optimistic at the moment.

CHAPTER THREE

DYLAN HATED HIS MOTHER'S new house the moment he saw it. Cathleen held the steering wheel of her Jeep with both hands, even though she'd already turned off the ignition. He supposed she was giving him time to take it all in.

The modern, California-style stucco three-story, with its triple garage and red clay-tile roof, stuck out like a monstrosity. An affront to the neighborhood of rustic, A-framed structures built of natural products like cedar and stone.

"Looks like a bloody movie set. I'm surprised they don't have fake palm trees lining the drive." Dylan jumped lightly from the passenger seat, his right hand automatically reaching to his left shoulder, protecting his injury from the jolt.

"Hard to imagine anything more different from your home on the ranch, isn't it?"

He just shook his head. The large, traditional log house where he'd grown up was practically museum quality. Generations of McLeans had taken loving care of the original structure, preserving architectural integrity during subsequent expansions and modernizing.

Dylan hung back, waiting for Cathleen to precede him along the brick path to the front entrance. A minute or so after she'd rung the doorbell, he leaned over her shoulder and pressed the buzzer impatiently several more times.

"I told you we should have called."

Cathleen toed her brown riding boot against the edge of a raised planter. The row of small globe cedars planted within looked dry and spindly. That surprised him. His mother was a formidable gardener.

Still no one answered the door. Bored, Dylan opened the mailbox and began sorting through the letters and flyers.

"What are you doing?"

"Just passing time." Leaning against the stucco wall, he noted the return address on one manila envelope, then replaced the package in the mailbox.

Cathleen stepped back impatiently. "Let's go. She's not going to let us in."

"Not so fast." Dylan hooked her at the waist, stopping her midstride. "Let me try the door."

He put a hand to the pewter handle and it immediately swung open. He gave her a wink. "Well?"

"We can't—"

As he pulled her over the threshold, a white cat

made an attempt to dart outside. Dylan caught the feline with one hand, then nudged the door shut with the heel of his boot.

"Mom? I'm home!" His masculine voice was loud and incongruous in the sparse perfection of the two-story foyer. Archways led on either side to a living room and den. Ahead, polished wooden stairs coiled to the upper rooms.

He began to worry. Were the rumors right? Was his mother too ill to get out of bed? From what Cathleen and Jake had said, it didn't seem likely that she was out.

About to march up the stairs, he paused at the sound of a door closing from one of the upper rooms. The white cat scampered out of Dylan's arms and bolted around the corner.

Finally, a slender feminine form appeared at the top of the stairs. "Where's Crystal?"

The white cat reappeared from its hiding place, zooming up the stairs to Rose Strongman's waiting arms.

"There you are, precious. You scared me. I heard the door and was afraid you'd run outside."

Rose began to descend the stairs. Dylan felt strange standing there; he wasn't sure if his mother had even seen him. In a way it was good. Frankly, he needed the moment to gather his composure.

He'd always thought of his mother as delicate. But dressed in a silk housecoat wrapped tightly around a too-narrow waist, Rose Strongman, née McLean, was now fragile to the point of brittleness. She had to have lost fifteen pounds, at least, since he'd seen her last. Her auburn hair had gone gray, and her skin sagged in grooves around her eyes, nose and mouth.

The changes were nothing unusual for a woman in her seventies or eighties. But his mother was fifty-seven.

As she came closer, Dylan saw more. The trembling in her hands, the watery film over her pale blue eyes, the crooked line of lipstick tracing a once-smiling mouth.

His mother had hurt him badly when she'd told him that she held him responsible for Jilly's death. The night before his and Cathleen's scheduled wedding she'd said he had no right marrying a wonderful girl like Cathleen and tainting her future with his past. She'd intimated that they'd all be much happier if he just made himself scarce.

Knowing that the source of these opinions was his stepfather, Max, hadn't helped him deal with the pain of her attack. He just couldn't understand why she would believe her husband over her own son. Couldn't she recognize manipulation when she saw it?

Dylan had stored up a lot of resentment toward his mother. Now he forgot all of it and just held out his arms.

"Mom…"

"Dylan?" Rose paused, which was a good thing, because otherwise she might have tumbled down the stairs. She transferred the cat to one arm and clung to the banister with the other. "You've come back."

"I have." He stood his ground and waited for the slightest sign that she was happy to see him.

"Why? This isn't your home anymore."

Dylan dropped his arms to his sides. He should've known. "Can't a son drop in to see his mother? I heard you've been under the weather."

Rose raised her chin. No faulting her posture. "I'm perfectly well."

Too concerned to bother with tact, he shook his head. "You don't look it."

"Don't be ridiculous." The words themselves were strident, but they lost their effect when delivered in Rose's wavering voice.

"Rose, you do seem a little weak," Cathleen said. "Would you like us to help you back to bed?"

"Of course not. Please stop this. I hate fussing." She squinted, making Dylan wonder if the moisture he'd seen over her eyes was really early-stage cataracts. "Is that you, Cathleen Shannon? What in the world are *you* doing here?"

Cathleen eyed him quickly before answering. "I've been meaning to drop by for a visit. You don't get out much anymore. In fact, I don't think I've seen you since—''

Rose blinked rapidly. ''You're right. I don't go out anymore. How can I?'' She focused on Dylan. ''A mother has to take responsibility for how her children turn out.''

A sickening mixture of guilt and anger twisted Dylan's gut. His mother had become a recluse because of him? Instinctively his hands curled into fists, but there was no one to fight. A good strong left couldn't touch public opinion.

''Can we just sit down and talk for a minute?'' Cathleen suggested.

It was a good idea, but where? Glancing around, he couldn't see a place to get comfortable. All the rooms looked formal and pristine. ''Maybe in the kitchen?''

In the old days, when his father was alive, his family had practically lived around the old oak table that had sat by the window overlooking the east pasture. Following Rose to the back of the house, he wasn't surprised to see a new wrought-iron set in the showpiece kitchen. The entire room was beyond what he could've imagined. Custom cherry cabinetry, beautiful marble countertops and restaurant-quality stainless steel appliances all vied for attention in the large space.

''Please sit down.'' A trace of Rose's old hospitality surfaced as she beckoned them to the thickly cushioned chairs.

"How about I put on the kettle for some tea," Cathleen offered.

"Good idea," Dylan said. "Maybe I can find some crackers and cheese to go with that." His mother was so frail he wondered if she ever ate. She used to have a good appetite, a love of delicious food. He went to the built-in fridge and saw no shortage of supplies. He picked out a nice hunk of Brie.

"No!" his mother said. "That's for Max. He likes it with a glass of wine after dinner."

Oh really? Dylan eyed the trash compactor, but Cathleen snatched the cheese from his hands before he dared. She returned the Brie to the fridge and substituted Cheddar.

He pulled himself together. It was only cheese, after all. Crackers were in the pantry next to the fridge. While Cathleen prepared the tea, he sliced the cheddar and placed it on a plate with the Wheat Thins.

His mother was staring out the window, holding the cat, stroking her compulsively. For a second Dylan had the uncomfortable feeling that she wasn't quite there mentally. And then abruptly, she focused on him, with eyes suddenly bright and alert.

"Why'd you come back, Dylan?"

"Cathleen asked me the same question last night. I'm beginning to think no one wants me."

"Really? You're so sensitive," Cathleen muttered.

"It was safer when you were gone," Rose added.

"They aren't going to arrest me, Mom," he said, then realized that wasn't what she'd meant. "For Max, you mean?"

During his extended stay at the hospital in Reno, it had occurred to him that his departure from Canmore had been very convenient for Max. With Dylan gone, Max had full control. Of the ranch, the money...and Rose.

His mother's expression started to turn blank again, as if she'd decided to opt out of the conversation. Cathleen reached for the woman's pale hand and changed the subject. She brought Rose up-to-date with news about former neighbors, then the results of a recent fund-raiser given by the horticultural society.

Gradually, Rose began to relax. A couple of times she even smiled. How could she not, with Cathleen's outrageous stories? Dylan wondered if she was just making them up, then decided it didn't really matter. Just hearing her talk was enough. For his mother, anyway.

Him, he wanted more. But given Cathleen's frosty attitude, it was hard to believe that there had once been a time when she'd returned his smiles and welcomed his touches. Now those days felt as distant as something he'd read about in a book or seen in a movie.

Cathleen had poured his tea black and strong, just the way he liked it. He took a sip, then focused on his mother. Cathleen was chatting on about an editorial she must have read in the local paper that week. There was a spark of pleasure in Rose's eyes as she listened. Dylan wondered what else brightened his mother's days. Her cat, obviously. But were there any people she still connected with? Friends from the old days?

Not likely, since she didn't seem to have heard any of the news Cathleen was telling her.

Rose took a sip of her tea and nodded at something Cathleen said. Gradually, she let her gaze slide over to her son. Seeing the resulting frown didn't make him feel very good.

He couldn't stop himself from bringing up the subject again. "You know I didn't hurt Jilly, don't you, Mom?"

For a moment he caught a glimpse of something soft and warm. The woman who had read him stories and baked him cookies and kissed his scraped knees was still inside there. But almost as soon as the softening happened, it disappeared. His mother's gaze became vague again, and her mouth tightened with anxiety.

"You shouldn't have caused trouble for Max,"

she said. "If only you could have left well enough alone."

"Max is the one causing the problems. Dad would never have allowed those wells to be drilled on the Bar M."

"Your father isn't here anymore."

No. He sure as hell wasn't. "What's going on with the ranch?"

She shook her head.

"I heard you hired Danny Mizzoni to look after it."

"The mayor of Canmore ought to live in town," Rose said weakly.

Cathleen's glance showed the same concern he felt. His mother was talking like a robot. And he sure as hell knew who'd programmed her.

"The ranch isn't even being operated anymore, is it?" Dylan tried not to sound bitter, but the news he'd heard from both Jake and Cathleen sickened him to the core. Apparently the herd had been sold, as well as most of the equipment.

"It's for the best."

He ignored Cathleen's restraining hand on his arm. "I'd like to know what Dad—"

"Your father is dead. Max is the head of this family now."

She couldn't have said anything that would have infuriated him more. "Max has nothing to do with me. And he doesn't have any business making decisions that concern my land."

"It's not your land, Dylan."

"I'm a McLean, aren't I? You know Dad meant for me and Jake to own the ranch one day."

Rose tightened her lips. "When I heard about Jilly, I redid my will. After I die, everything goes to Max. And when he dies, it passes on to James."

Dylan heard Cathleen gasp. "You can't mean that..." He sputtered and grabbed tight to the hand that had just reached out to him. Cathleen's hand.

"Mother, that land means everything to me. If you want to give half to the Strongmans and the rest to me and Jake, I'm willing to talk about that. But you can't cut us out completely."

It couldn't be legal, could it? If only his father had bequeathed the land directly to him! But his dad's simple will had left everything to his wife, on the understanding that she would pass the land on to Dylan and Jake when it was her turn to go. It had sounded simple enough when his father had sat the three of them around the kitchen table to discuss it. Of course his father could never have anticipated Max Strongman entering their lives.

"I need to have that ranch," he told his mother now. "It's my birthright."

His mother truly seemed torn. "Why did you hurt that girl?" she asked sadly.

He'd told her once. He wouldn't say it again.

But Cathleen didn't have the same scruples. "In your heart, Rose, you have to know Dylan didn't harm Jilly. He could never do such a thing."

Hearing Cathleen defend him, Dylan felt a weird, fluttering sensation in his gut. She sounded so sincere, so heartfelt. Did she really trust him that much?

Rose's mouth trembled. "You forget that Max was present that day. He saw it all. Out of respect for me, he didn't tell the RCMP. But he saw Dylan shoot that girl—"

"He did not!" The dirty lying bastard... Dylan shot up from his chair, spilling some of his tea. Rose cowered, as if she expected him to strike her. But why? Unless she'd become conditioned to react that way to an angry man.

"Max wouldn't lie to me," Rose said softly.

Dylan held his hands close to his body and spoke gently. "*I'm* not the one who hits you, Mom. And I'm not the one lying to you. One day, I hope you believe me."

DYLAN DIDN'T TALK on the way back to the B and B and Cathleen understood. She drove with the window down, her elbow propped on the ledge. Sometimes a brisk cleansing wind was the most you could ask for in a day.

At Larch Lodge, Poppy had lunch waiting. Cathleen didn't have the heart to admit she had no appetite. Since the table was set for three, Dylan sat, too.

Cathleen pressed her fork into the quiche, then tried her first bite, aware that Poppy was eyeing her anxiously. The crust was buttery and light; the chopped carrots, onions, potatoes and celery, moist and curry flavored.

"Perfect," Cathleen said, and Dylan concurred.

Poppy smiled. She sat and watched them eat for almost a minute, without taking a taste. Finally, she sighed.

"You *say* it's good, but you don't seem to be enjoying it."

"It's not the food, Poppy." Cathleen laid down her fork. "It's Dylan's mother. Our visit didn't go well."

"Oh?"

"She's obviously not healthy. She's way too thin and…high-strung."

"But she was pleased to see her son?"

Dylan, too, set down his fork. Murmuring an apology, he stalked off to the porch.

Cathleen raised her eyebrows at Poppy.

"I guess that answers my question. How sad. Family belong together."

"Not always," Cathleen replied, thinking of her no-account father. "In this case, though, I agree. Rose could use her son's support, but Max has poi-

soned her mind against him. He's convinced her
that Dylan shot Jilly.''

"I see." Poppy's forehead collapsed into wrinkles, a sign, Cathleen had learned, of warring emotions. The older woman shook her head, then came
to a conclusion.

"Kelly called this morning," she said. "When
she heard you were out with Dylan she became very
perturbed, and I must admit she convinced me that
you need to be very careful. Are you certain you
can discount Rose's opinion of Dylan so easily?
While I'd be the first to admit that mothers don't
always know their children as well as they think
they do, they usually have a fundamental understanding of their character. If she thinks Dylan
could have shot Jilly…''

"Only because of her husband. Max Strongman
is very domineering.'' After today, she was almost
positive he was abusive, as well. He'd been physical with Dylan, she knew, back in the early days
when the two had lived under one roof. But she'd
never guessed he might be hurting his own wife.

"Well, Kelly seems to think—''

"Poppy—'' Cathleen held up her hand ''—I love
my sister dearly, but she's a worrier. What does she
think is going to happen? That Dylan will murder
me in the middle of the night?''

Poor Poppy quaked a little at that comment. "Oh
dear, I hope not. Perhaps locks on the bedroom door

wouldn't be a bad idea. But truly, I think her main concern is for your...for your heart.''

She'd spoken her last words tentatively, as if she sensed that Cathleen might object to this, most of all. Which only proved how well Poppy was getting to know her.

''Poppy, do I look like a fool? My heart is perfectly safe.''

''He's a good-looking man. And a charismatic one.''

''On the surface, yes,'' Cathleen agreed. ''But my mother taught me that it's what men *do,* not *say,* that counts. My father is the perfect example. He always said he loved my mother, but every time she had a baby he ran out on her, only to return several months later. Two times Mom let him get away with this. Then, finally, when she was pregnant with Kelly, she told him that if he took off again, he shouldn't bother coming back.''

''And he left?''

''You bet.''

''That must have been very hard for your mother.''

''Her mistake was not kicking him out the first time.''

Back came those wrinkles. ''You and Kelly wouldn't have been born, then.''

Cathleen had to concede that point. ''I guess we were lucky our mother had a soft streak. With apologies to any unborn children out there, I don't agree.''

"Isn't that a little harsh? People make mistakes. It's part of the human condition.''

"Depends what you call a mistake. Coming home late, forgetting a birthday—those are mistakes. Running out on a mother and her newborn baby…'' *Not showing up for your own wedding…* "Well, that seems like more than a mistake to me.''

The hesitation in Poppy's smile told Cathleen she hadn't quite convinced the older woman of her philosophy.

"Listen, Poppy. I'm going to see how Dylan's doing. Will you leave the dishes for me to do later?''

Cathleen pushed through the screen door and found Dylan in one of her willow chairs, Kip at his feet. Slouched back, with his hat covering his face, he made the perfect picture of ease, but she knew better. Briefly, she rested a hand on his good shoulder, and found the muscles as tense as she'd expected. She went to the stairs and sat with her back against the railing, facing him.

All morning she'd been fighting the way the man drew her in. Each time their glances connected, her chest tightened in an oh-so-familiar—and oh-so-dangerous—way. The emotion—the intensity and hopelessness of it—reminded her of her high school years. Dylan was three years her senior and hadn't deigned to notice her until she'd turned eighteen. When he'd finally woken up and taken stock of the middle Shannon girl all the boys were talking about, they'd quickly become friends. She'd been too young for their relationship to be more than that, and he'd understood.

She'd enjoyed dating boys her own age, playing the field. Her mother had warned all three of her daughters not to make the mistake of marrying too young. And Dylan had been content to wait.

On her twenty-sixth birthday, everything had changed. Dylan didn't want to wait anymore, and neither did she. All along, she'd known he was the one. And at last the time was right.

That was when their relationship had taken on such passionate intensity that she'd realized just how inconsequential all her previous romantic entanglements had been. Two years later they'd become engaged.

Inseparable.

Until he took off the morning of their wedding.

Slowly, Dylan's right hand rose. He lifted his hat and settled it back on his head, then gazed off toward the mountains that dominated the southern boundary of her property. The peaks were old friends to Cathleen, and she knew they offered the same sense of timeless serenity to him.

Dylan took a chest-expanding breath. ''He's hitting her.''

The stark, simple statement pierced the afternoon quiet. "I know. I saw some bruises on her leg when her housecoat shifted." They'd been the multicolored kind, ugly and raw-looking. At the time, Cathleen hadn't been sure what could have caused such an injury. Now she was.

"I wanted to pick her up and carry her out of that house," Dylan said.

"That wouldn't work. Rose has to *want* to leave."

"I know."

"When did the abuse start, do you think?"

Dylan frowned. "I was sixteen when they married and I left home at eighteen. During those years I was so busy fighting with Max I didn't pay much attention to how he was getting along with my mother. She always backed *him* whenever we had a disagreement, so I guess I assumed she was happy in her marriage. I'm almost positive he wasn't hurting her then."

Dylan had told her about those days before, but he'd glossed over the bad parts. "Why do you think Max disliked you so much?"

"I used to ask myself that question all the time. He'd criticize everything about me, from the way I rode a horse to the way I fed the cattle... Finally, I realized there was just no winning with him. Once I gave up caring, it didn't seem to matter so much anymore.

"And that's when I started feeling more sorry for James than I did for myself. Max didn't fight with his own son the way he did me, but he was always belittling and caustic, which in a way must've been worse. Especially since James tried so hard to please the son of a gun."

Cathleen knew the situation had been bad enough that after grade twelve graduation, Dylan had been more than ready to move out and rent a place of his own. At first his plan had been to keep working at the Thunder Bar M, but the fighting between him and Max had made that impossible. Eventually he'd been forced to accept a foreman position on a property about fifty kilometers closer to Calgary.

"Max has always been domineering," Cathleen said, remembering the few social occasions when she and Dylan had been invited to dine at the ranch. "But your mother seemed to take his demanding ways in stride."

"I guess she was used to having a strong husband. She and Dad had a traditional marriage. When it came to ranch business, his word was law in our house. But he really loved her, and at heart had a real gentleness. Max, unfortunately, hasn't got a soft side. At least not that I've ever seen."

"He's been a controversial mayor, but he has his loyal supporters."

"Yeah, I bet he does. People with an eye on profits rather than the future of the land." Dylan planted the heels of his cowboy boots into the planks of the porch and started his chair rocking. "But you raise a good point. With Max's stature in this town, I'm going to have a hell of a time convincing the law that he was responsible for Jilly's death."

"I know you hate him, and I know you have your reasons. But how can you be so sure that he was the one who shot her?"

Dylan laughed bitterly. "I've had two years to mull this over. Ask yourself two questions. Who benefited when that demonstration broke up? And who had the most to gain by framing *me* for the crime?"

"I know Max had his motives. And I admit he's a bully capable of violence. But would he really stoop to murder? I think we need to find out more about him. His past, before he married your mother."

"Darlin', I couldn't agree more."

Cathleen thought a moment. "Maureen might be able to help." Her elder sister, recently widowed, was going through a bad patch right now, but as a lawyer she'd have the kind of connections they'd need.

Dylan stopped rocking. He leaned forward, his arms on his thighs. "You figure she'd talk to me if I phoned her?"

Maureen, like Kelly, could be very protective.

And strong willed. Hanging up on Dylan wouldn't be beyond her. "Maybe *I* should call her first."

"And would you come to Calgary with me?"

Oh Lord. She'd virtually trapped herself into saying yes. "You've got to understand this is all about proving what really happened to Jilly."

"In other words, you're not just looking for excuses to spend time with me."

"You wish."

"Damn right I do." Dylan's gray eyes lost their twinkle. "But for now, it's all about that night in Thunder Valley."

If only he'd thought this way two years ago! But it was too late now for regrets. "Who else was there, Dylan? You and your cousin Jake. And, of course, Max and his son, and Jilly and her father. Do I know any of the others?"

"You do. Hang on a minute. They published a list in the *Leader*. I have it in my pack."

Dylan went into the house and came back with two coffees as well as a sheet of folded paper. "I already added cream," he said, passing her one of the mugs and then half sitting on the white railing next to her.

"Thanks." For a disorienting moment, she remembered what it had felt like to be part of a couple who'd been together long enough to be aware of each other's tastes and preferences. She knew, for instance, that Dylan's coffee was black. Without checking, she could've identified the label on his jeans, his shirt, his cowboy hat…

"I could read you the names, but you might as well look this over yourself." He handed her the fragile, yellowed paper. She unfolded it once, twice, then ran an eye down the typed names. Heading the list was Max Strongman, followed by his son, James.

"Max was entertaining some of the oil company officials that afternoon, wasn't he?"

"Yes, at a big Western-style barbecue. Conrad Beckett and his daughter were there, as well as several other executives from Beckett Oil and Gas." Dylan pointed to their names, then trailed his finger down the list. "A couple of bankers and a representative from an accounting firm in Calgary."

"Where was your mother?" Cathleen wondered, not seeing any mention of Rose.

"Inside the kitchen, helping the caterer make salads, stuff like that. When our group showed up, she came outside briefly, but Max ordered her back into the house."

Cathleen could well imagine. "And the group you'd gotten together…?"

"An ad hoc thing, as you know. Jake was with me, of course, along with a few of his buddies who care pretty deeply about protecting the wildlife corridor along the Bow River. I also had some ranchers organized…."

She knew, or had heard of, most of these people. One name stood out. "Mick Mizzoni was there, too?"

"Yeah. I thought he might give us some favorable coverage in the *Leader*. Little did I guess just how big the story was going to be."

Cathleen counted. Thirty-one people. "If only just one of them had been watching the right person at the right time…"

"'If only' can be a dangerous game to play. It can make a man crazy, if he lets it."

She twisted to see his eyes more clearly. Over the years she'd learned to read the moods implicit in their almost infinite shades of gray. She'd seen them twinkle like polished silver when he was happy, or turn as cloudy as nearby Lac des Arc during spring runoff when he was sad. Now their dark hue told her he was serious.

"I suppose you regret going out to the ranch that night."

"I regret a hell of a lot more than that." He focused on her. "I shouldn't have left the way I did, Cathleen. I never wrote, but that doesn't mean I didn't think about you. I did. Every day. Almost every second, it felt like sometimes."

"You apologized last night," she reminded him, lowering her head to catch a perfect view of the floorboards she'd stained by hand two years ago.

She counted the knots rather than focus on how deeply felt Dylan's words sounded.

"Yeah, but I made a mess of it. I was nervous."

"You?" Never had she known a man with Dylan's confidence.

"Hard to imagine, huh?" He stretched out his legs till his boots touched the bottom rung of the stairs. "But it happens to be true. Want to know something else that's true?"

She shook her head, but he answered, anyway. "I still love you, darlin'. That's one thing that hasn't changed."

She'd hoped he wouldn't actually say those words. Hearing them now, she felt only anger. "You don't know what it means to love a woman, Dylan."

"I'd like a chance to dispute that." He leaned in close, and the smell of him brought back such intense memories she almost caved right there and then. *Kiss me, Dylan.*

She jumped to her feet, not able to trust her own feelings and reactions. Even *thinking* about kissing Dylan was dangerous. She'd be lost if she ever allowed it to happen.

Dylan stood, backing her against the stair railing. "I *do* love you."

Cathleen leaned into the wooden support behind her, her heart galloping. "You had the chance to marry me and you chose to walk."

He put a hand to the side of her head. "I'm sorry."

She yanked away from his touch, hating how much it affected her. When he was this close it was so hard to think clearly. *Strike one,* she reminded herself. Playing by her rules, he'd had his opportunity and he'd blown it.

What she needed was distance—it was what they *both* needed. But Dylan didn't seem to think so. He took her hand, folding it warmly inside his. "Let's go for a walk. Just let me be with you for a while."

With relief, she recalled previously made plans for the evening. "I can't. I've got to get ready to go out."

In a flash, the gray of his eyes turned dull. "Let me guess. You've got a date." He was quiet for a moment, then he swore. "It's worse than that, isn't it? You're going out with *James.*"

"Yes."

She'd known he'd see the outing as a betrayal, and after the day they'd spent together and the bombshell Rose had delivered about the will, she didn't blame him. Her relationship with James, the man who would eventually own the Thunder Bar M Ranch unless Rose changed her will, had to sting at least a little. Cathleen didn't want to be cruel, especially when her interest in James was mild at best.

But maybe going out with James, at least this one more time, would give Dylan the message that their love was truly over. And maybe it would give her the same message.

CHAPTER FOUR

CATHLEEN FOUND James Strongman a bit of a puzzle. He'd been blessed with exceptional, classical good looks and a tall, slender frame. He could be pleasant company, and she'd found him a handy companion for parties where guests were expected to be sociable. But on the occasions when just the two of them were out for dinner, he bordered, unfortunately, on the dull side.

In fact, she'd almost come to the conclusion that he was a little slow. One evening he'd voiced a strong, well-reasoned opinion in support of free trade that had impressed her—until she'd read a quote from Max Strongman in the *Leader* that was almost identical.

So it wasn't just Dylan's reappearance in Canmore that had her thinking it was time to put an end to their dates. But she had to admit it was a contributing factor.

Actually telling James about her decision wouldn't be fun. These things never were. She waited until after their movie in Banff, then invited him home for a drink, which she poured in her study. Dylan was out—he'd asked to borrow her Jeep. In the kitchen, Poppy was experimenting with her favorite fudge recipes.

"I hear Dylan's back in town," James commented after she handed him his Scotch and water.

"Yes." She turned her back to add a piece of birch to the fire she'd started as soon as they'd entered the room.

"And staying here. With you."

She heard a creak from the leather chair and knew James had stood. Turning, she almost bumped into his chest.

"This is a bed-and-breakfast, James. He's renting the room next to Poppy's."

James ran a hand down the perfectly chiseled plane of his cheek, then across the square angle of his jaw. He was wearing a black turtleneck with black slacks—a sophisticated look out of place in the outdoorsy mountain town of Canmore, where most men considered they were dressing up when they removed their sporting gear in favor of a pair of khakis and a clean shirt.

"I don't understand how you can have that man under your roof after what he did to you. Not to mention *Jilly Beckett.*"

Cathleen stared past him into the orange-blue flames of the fire. "Dylan didn't kill that girl."

"You don't believe that."

When she didn't answer, James changed tack.

"If you do, you're the only one in town who does. Anyway, there's still the fact that he left you high and dry on your wedding day."

"That was years ago. Why does everyone have to make such a big deal out of it?" Cathleen circled to the back of the sofa, where she could face both the fire and her guest. She hadn't poured herself a drink and was only waiting for him to finish his before delivering her short farewell speech, then showing him the door.

"What about the black eye he gave his mother the night before he left town?"

"You and I both know who really hit Rose that night, don't we, James?"

Her guest covered his confusion by coughing, but Cathleen saw through the ploy. James probably knew much more than any of them gave him credit for. She wondered how much he'd be willing to share with her.

"Have you heard that Rose cut Dylan from her will?" She'd hoped Rose's threat had been merely that. But James was quick to confirm the point.

"Wouldn't you, in her shoes? That land is wasted on ranching. Dylan just doesn't see the potential that my father and I—"

"Do you mean the oil wells?"

"Not just that. The recreational property market is so hot right now. If that land was subdivided, we could market the mountain and river views in no time flat.''

This was the first Cathleen had heard of any development plans. ''You can't be serious!'' Seeing the family ranch chopped into parcels, trees razed, ground stripped by bulldozers, would really kill Dylan.

''We definitely are. We've got a firm in Calgary working on the plans. It's going to be a father-son venture,'' he added proudly.

Well, wasn't that sweet. ''You know what, James? I think it's time you left.''

''What's wrong?''

Cathleen took the empty glass from his hand. ''I don't think we should see each other anymore. We have different priorities in life.''

He blinked. ''But we've been dating for months. I thought things were going so well. You know, I'm not interested in any woman but you.''

A minute ago, she would've sworn all he cared about was dollar signs. Now...hell, was the man sincere? ''James, you'll find someone else.''

''You don't understand....''

The purring of an approaching engine, accompanied by the sound of gravel crunching under tires, told her Dylan was back. Maybe now James would leave. But if he heard the vehicle, if he guessed who it might be, he didn't seem concerned. She sensed him regrouping as he handed over his glass.

"How about one more Scotch, Cathleen? Let's talk this over."

"You really shouldn't have another drink. Not when you're driving. Besides, there's nothing for us to talk about. I've made up my mind."

"A coffee, then?"

"Why postpone the inevitable? It would be better if you just went home."

"But I can't do that! I'm sorry I complained about Dylan. Let's just keep seeing each other. We were getting along fine before he showed up."

Was there a tactful way to tell a man that he would never inspire love and longing the way another had once done? She didn't think so.

"You want children, don't you?"

"Children? James—"

"Well, so do I. I bet we'd have beautiful children, Cathleen."

He held out his hand and she avoided his touch by going to pour that second Scotch, taking care to make it mostly water.

"This property of yours—of course you know it butts up to the far corner of the McLean ranch. Can you imagine how rich we'd be if we developed all along this stretch of Thunder Creek?"

Cathleen's sympathy for the man vanished with a flash of insight. Her land. That was why he'd been so adamant about dating her. Probably his father had masterminded this romance. She felt a fool for not having caught on sooner.

About to tell James to take a jump in the aforementioned creek, she was stopped by a voice from the doorway.

"I see you're a real long-term planner, James." It was Dylan, hand propped against the door frame, one booted foot hooked around the other.

James swiveled and his hand jerked, spilling Scotch onto the Turkish rug at his feet. "Damn it, Dylan! Where did you come from?"

"Never mind about me. I want to know what was going on *here*. Correct me if I'm wrong, but it sounded like you were leading up to asking my fiancée if she wanted to marry *you!*"

Cathleen gasped. Her blood came to an instant boil. All the anger she'd been reining in since Dylan had dropped back into her life surfaced in one hot, intense flood of emotion.

"Don't call me your fiancée."

"But, darlin'..."

"And stop calling me *darling!*" She grabbed a pillow from the sofa and squeezed tight, then whirled on James, who was telling Dylan that he couldn't come back after two years and expect to have any rights to the woman he'd left at the altar.

"Am I an oil well now? No man has *rights* to me! And certainly not *you two!*"

James's veneer-thin confidence cracked under attack. "Ca-Cathleen?" He backed himself against a wall, and somehow, his capitulation only made her more furious.

"As for you." She whipped around to face Dylan, knowing she was about to completely lose it and powerless to stop herself. "I am *sick* of your conceited attitude. Who do you think you are, interfering in my private life?"

Dylan backed off a little, but not so much that she missed seeing the beginning of a smirk pull at the corner of his mouth.

That smirk did it. Rage drowned out the last of her resolve. She threw the pillow with all her might, and her anger flared again when he simply reached out with one hand and caught it. She grabbed at a magazine on the coffee table and threw that, too. Then her boots, which she'd kicked off earlier and left lying by the desk.

Dylan dodged each missile, bending this way and that. If he was still smirking, she was too furious to see.

"I am *not* your fiancée. You ran out on me and never called and never wrote...."

She was beside him now, pushing her fists against his chest. "Do you know how that felt? Waiting day after day—"

"Cath—"

She picked up the pillow again and crushed it to his face, smothering his words. "Oh, shut up. You were laughing all the time, weren't you? Just another silly prank, cutting out on your wedding day. Then coming back *two years later* and pretending we were still going to get married. You probably thought I'd be that desperate, didn't you?''

Pummeling him with the pillow, she aimed her shots lower and lower as he sank slowly to the floor. She knew she wasn't really hurting him, but it felt so good to lash out at last. ''I am *not* going to marry you, Dylan. Is that clear? I wish I'd never had the misfortune to meet you....''

She kicked him then, catching the top of his cowboy boot with her bare foot.

''Ow! Damn it, Dylan, don't you dare laugh!''

Amazingly, he didn't. But the combination of passion and tenderness in his eyes—even as he held his good arm in a protective arch above his face—made her stop to catch her breath.

She dropped the cushion. What was she doing? She had to get control of herself. Bending slightly, her hands on her thighs, she took several breaths. Finally, feeling human again, she turned to James.

''Just to make sure you're perfectly clear on this,'' she said. ''There will be no marriage, no riverside development, no beautiful children. Got it?''

James nodded wordlessly.

''Good.'' She straightened her back.

''Can I get up now?'' Dylan looked ridiculous

with his hand still raised tentatively to his face. When she said nothing, he eased himself upright. Bypassing Cathleen cautiously, he reached a hand to James and pulled him from the wall, then made a show of dusting off his shoulders.

"I'd almost forgotten what a good temper you throw. Comes from having Irish blood on both sides," he explained to James. "I thought maybe she'd grown out of it, though."

Cathleen pushed aside a wave of embarrassment. "I was provoked. You both had it coming. You're just lucky the fire poker wasn't handy."

Damn, but she distrusted the confidence that was back in his eyes, in his smile. "I meant every word I said, Dylan."

"I know, darlin', and I don't blame you one bit. Now, do you think we should plan another big wedding, or try for something a little smaller this time?"

DYLAN REALIZED HE'D GONE too far—yet again—but Cathleen didn't get angry this time. She just sighed heavily as she collected her boots and slipped them back on her feet.

"Chocolate fudge, anyone?" Poppy showed up at the doorway with a plate of richly scented candies. "I have maple walnut and chocolate pecan." She narrowed her eyes at James. "You're not allergic to nuts, are you?"

"No, ma'am." He took what he'd been offered and shoved the entire piece in his mouth. Dylan doubted if he tasted a thing. A few chews, then he swallowed and grabbed his hat.

"I'd better be leaving."

"Good idea," Dylan agreed. Cathleen shot him one of those "go to hell" looks he remembered from arguments past. He didn't mind. It was much better than those "who were you again?" looks he'd been receiving up until now.

"I'll leave these candies here," Poppy said, placing the plate atop a stack of papers on Cathleen's desk. She seemed to have no trouble reading the charged situation. "Come on, James. I'll reacquaint you with the front door. Hardly anyone seems to use it around here."

Once the two were gone, Dylan picked up the cushion from the floor and tossed it back on the sofa, then restacked the magazines on the table. But even after the room was tidied, Cathleen still looked ticked. She was leaning against the door frame, and if steam had been coming out the top of her head, he wouldn't have been surprised.

He passed her the plate of fudge. When she didn't respond, he put it back on the desk and helped himself to a piece of the maple walnut. The sugar dissolved almost before it hit his tongue. He murmured appreciatively, even though the fudge was definitely too sweet for his taste.

Walking over to the window, he tried to see if James had left yet. When he saw the man step off the porch toward his car, he felt a brief lightening in his chest.

"Well, I hope we've seen the last of him," he said, dusting his hands on his jeans.

"Oh you do, do you?"

"What's the matter, darlin'? Still cross?" He shouldn't feel so pleased with himself. His satisfaction showed in his face, his posture, his tone of voice. It would only make her angrier.

But he couldn't help it. Cathleen had lost her temper. Really lost it, throwing stuff and shouting and swearing just like the good old days. In a day full of disappointment, it was the one bright spot. Now she could tell him she didn't care for him anymore until she was blue in the face.

And he'd know she was lying.

By MONDAY MORNING Cathleen had put the scene in the study behind her. So she'd lost her temper. It could've happened to anyone. The amazing thing was that she'd held herself in check this long!

The only problem was, since her tirade her anger against Dylan had lost its edge, leaving her with an unsettling emptiness. Because while it had felt good at the time, it hadn't changed a thing. No amount of shouting or blaming on her part, no amount of repentant shrugs on Dylan's, could alter their past.

And here she was, planning to spend the entire day in Calgary in order to help the cad. Was she certifiable, or what? Last night she'd called Maureen to set up an appointment. Any moment now, they'd be getting into the Jeep. She glared at Dylan over the breakfast table, feeling somehow outmaneuvered. He still bore that slightly smug expression from last night. The poor fool seemed to think that lashing out at him had been some sort of admission of love. What a load of crap.

In a twisted way, Dylan almost enjoyed the bad vibes emanating from Cathleen's midnight-blue eyes. Her earlier disdain and indifference had been much harder for him to deal with than outright anger followed by a case of the sulks. Contributing to his good mood was the prospect of an entire day in her company. Cathleen had outfitted herself in red cowboy boots, a flared tan skirt and a smashing red leather jacket. She would draw eyes wherever they went. Most especially his.

He washed breakfast dishes while she ran upstairs to do a few last-minute girlie things. He noticed lipstick and the scent of perfume when she returned.

"Let's get this over with," she said.

He tried not to smile, guessing she wouldn't be impressed if he acted too pleased about the situation. In the Jeep he made a suggestion. "Think we could manage a quick detour to the Bar M before we head into Calgary? I haven't seen the place in the light of day yet.''

Cathleen paused, her hand on the key. ''The ranch? I'm not sure that's a good idea.''

He reached across the console, placing his hand over hers and then twisting her fingers to the right. The engine hummed. ''Just drive, darlin'. We've got a busy day ahead of us.''

''What we've got ahead of us is trouble,'' Cathleen grumbled, but instead of taking the right to the Trans-Canada Highway, she took the left to the Bar M as he'd asked.

Cathleen slowed the Jeep as they passed over the cattle guard that marked the beginning of McLean property, then sped up for the last mile to the ranch house turnoff.

Dylan's heart swelled at the sight of the familiar curves of the hills, the proud stands of lodgepole pine and white spruce. The profile of the awesome mountain peaks that rose on either side of the valley were as unique to him as a fingerprint would be to an FBI agent. As a young boy he'd believed those mountains marked the very borders of the world.

The low green banks of Thunder Creek—a tributary of the Bow—made for the best grazing. To not see a single head of cattle there now, only a line of pump jacks sucking oil from the earth's innards, hurt. Dylan thought of his dad, as he always did when he saw these fields, picturing him in his dusty brown work hat, on the back of Rustler, his favorite quarter horse.

"Mind if I open the window?" he asked, eager to breathe in the very particular scents of autumn in the foothills.

"Go right ahead."

Fresh air blasted the small space, carrying with it a familiar mountain tang. He'd always loved September. The smells, the colors, the combination of warm sun and cooling air. Never was the sky so blue as it was at this time of year, a perfect foil for the golden leaves of the trembling aspen and balsam poplars.

"Missed all this?" Cathleen asked as she eased off on the accelerator.

"Hell, yes." He leaned forward in his seat, anticipating the turnoff to the ranch house. A small sign posted by the road warned tourists and hikers that this was private property. His throat tightened as they veered left onto packed dirt and gravel, the Jeep now jostling on the dried ruts like a jackrabbit.

A hundred meters farther, the wrought-iron gate, incorporating the ranch's brand—a bolt of lightning through the letter *M*—lay open. Dylan frowned at that sign of neglect as Cathleen slowed, anticipating the bend that would take them down to the ranch house.

His first glimpse of the house pained him. Paint peeled like wood curls from the trim around the windows and doors. The cedar buckets flanking both sides of the main entrance stood empty of flowers. A junked car suspended on cement blocks had been stripped of its tires, and who knew what else. His mother's pretty cotton curtains no longer hung in the windows, but some rags that might once have been sheets were tacked up at the corners. The only cheerful note was the colorful plastic toys scattered around the front porch.

"I should've guessed." Man, he felt old all of a sudden.

Cathleen braked, then both of them jumped to the ground. Leaning against the other side of the Jeep, Cathleen slanted her own critical eye on the place. "Wouldn't take long to whip into shape."

"I suppose." But would he get the chance? He bypassed the home where he'd grown up and headed toward the creek that ran about a hundred meters from the side of the house. Behind him, he could hear Cathleen's boots scuffing against the dirt and pebbles.

Soon they heard laughter, a child's shout. He glanced back at Cathleen.

"Danny's children. His wife's name is Sharon, I think. Haven't seen much of them since they moved in."

Dylan stopped to pick up a discarded whiskey bottle from the ground. Glancing off to the side, he saw more litter, most of it of the alcohol variety. "What the hell?"

"I've heard they have some pretty wild parties out here. Some nights over a dozen vehicles drive past the B and B."

"Great." He dropped the bottle and continued toward the playing children. Past a clump of silver willows, he spotted them. A little guy, not yet school-age, tossed a rock into the river. With the splash, the toddler sitting on a patch of grass nearby giggled.

Where the hell were the parents? He glanced at Cathleen and saw she was equally concerned.

"Dylan, that boy can't be more than four. And his sister is still in diapers." She raised her voice, "Hey, little boy! Careful not to fall in. There's a powerful current in that creek!"

The boy froze and stared.

"I'm your neighbor, Cathleen Shannon. And this guy here is Dylan McLean. Is your mom around?"

The boy, who'd been standing in water to his knees, stepped up onto the bank. He picked up his sister and held her close, as if afraid Cathleen and Dylan were going to snatch her. His gaze shot to the log house.

"Is your mom in there?" Dylan guessed.

The boy nodded slowly. "She's taking good care of us. We had a big breakfast. Eggs and bacon and lots of toast."

Somehow Dylan doubted that was the truth. He noticed the boy was in pajamas. The little girl just had a sweater over her diaper. The diaper, at least, appeared clean and fresh.

"That sounds real tasty," Cathleen said, coming up beside Dylan and planting a hand on his shoulder. Undoubtedly she was only cautioning him not to overreact in front of the kids. He didn't care what the reason. It was great to feel her touch.

"So where's your dad?" Dylan asked.

"Right behind you."

Cathleen and Dylan swiveled. Just rounding the willows was an extremely thin man of medium height. Mussed hair and an unshaven jaw gave the impression he'd just rolled out of bed. With a hangover.

"Daddy!" The toddler held out her arms.

Danny Mizzoni brushed past Dylan and Cathleen, then scooped up his child. She nestled right in, as though she was used to the cradle of his arms. Now Dylan could see her face. Blue eyes, round as a full moon, regarded him cautiously. The boy grabbed a stick and began scratching the ground with it.

"Dylan McLean, right?"

"You got it." Dylan squared his shoulders to eye Danny. They'd all grown up in Canmore, but Danny and his elder brother, Mick, had been younger than Dylan so they hadn't gone to school together or hung out with the same friends. That Mick and Danny had been social misfits hadn't helped much. Their mother had a reputation of the worst sort, although she'd left town a long time ago, Dylan recalled.

"Well, I'm sorry to have to tell you this, but your stepdad told me you weren't to come on this land anymore," Danny said.

Dylan focused in on pale blue eyes, ringed with red lines. Stepping closer, he caught the pungent aroma of stale alcohol. Feeling a new pressure from Cathleen's hand, he kept his voice low. "This isn't Max Strongman's land. Much as he likes to think it is."

"No," Danny agreed. "I reckon it's your mother's. But Max is the one who hired me to look after the place. And he's the one who told me—"

"Look after the place, huh?" Dylan glanced back at the neglected house. He still didn't understand why Max had hired a loser like Danny to safeguard such valuable property.

The little girl was the first to hear a second vehicle approach. She'd turned her round, smooth face to the lane just as Dylan was picking up the grumbling sound of a high-powered motor. He glanced at Danny to see if he was expecting someone.

"That'll be Max." Danny set the toddler on the

ground. "Billy, take your sister on up to the house. Get her a bowl of cereal or something."

Dylan could see the vehicle clearly now, a Land Rover. Whether the kids recognized it and didn't like the man they knew who drove it or whether they were just well behaved, they obeyed their father. The toddler didn't squawk as her father put her down but reached willingly for her big brother's hand.

Dylan shifted his attention to the man getting out of the Rover. Hell, it was Max all right. A big man, dressed in show-off Western clothes: new jeans and an embroidered cowboy shirt. His belly seemed to have expanded an inch for each year Dylan had been away. Now it extended over his belt, almost covering the large silver buckle. Tipped back on his head was a cream-colored Stetson. Dylan and his father had always favored Resistols.

Cathleen's fingers were clutching his bones like eagle talons. He'd been glad to have her reach out to him, but it *was* his injured shoulder she was perching on. "Uh, darlin'…" He winced a little, and she let go.

Leaning toward him, she whispered, "Don't let Max get to you."

He had just one grin to spare and he gave it to her. "Don't worry, darlin'. Cool as a cucumber—that's me."

"Since when?"

Dylan stepped forward to meet Max halfway. About three meters separated them when they both stopped. Dylan didn't offer his hand; neither did Max.

"So you're back." Max's glance slid to Danny, then to Cathleen. He touched the brim of his hat in acknowledgment. "Miss Shannon, of course you're welcome anytime, but Dylan, I think you should appreciate that your mother doesn't want you on this property anymore."

"I've got more right to be here than you do."

"Now, now, I don't want to start a fight. You know what a big disappointment you've been to Rose. Why make matters worse?"

Max took off his hat and squinted in Cathleen's direction. "I must say I'm sorry to see you here today, Miss Shannon. You're a beautiful woman, with your whole future in front of you. I'd hate for you to waste your possibilities on a man who isn't worthy."

Cathleen's back stiffened. Dylan waited for her to let Max know that she had no intention of wasting more than a day or two of her future on him.

"Thanks for the advice," she said. "But I happen to think I'm a fine judge of character."

Max's ruthless gaze shot back to Dylan. "And I happen to think a man should pay for his crimes."

Dylan's hand automatically formed a fist. But he managed to keep his cool. "So do I," he replied, staring steadily into his stepfather's narrowed eyes. "You know I didn't hurt that girl. But it sure suits your purposes to have everyone else think I'm guilty, doesn't it?" Especially his mother. Dylan's gut burned so hot it was a struggle to breathe.

"Still not willing to own up to your mistakes?"

"My only mistake was not running you off this property the first day I met you."

"Well, that's ironic, isn't it? Because now I'm asking you to leave and I've got every right to. Don't make me call the RCMP on this. You know they'll back me."

"You don't own this land."

Max just smiled, and Dylan knew what he was thinking. He might not be the legal owner yet, but as soon as Rose died, he would be. And with his mother's poor health, that unhappy day could arrive all too soon.

"If my mother dies, I'll contest her will."

"Come on, let's *go* Dylan." Cathleen took his hand and tried to lead him to her Jeep. He walked a few steps, before Max's voice stopped him cold.

"Good luck in court, boy. The fact that you'll be serving time for murder probably won't help your case any."

Damn it, the old man looked so smug. He *knew* something, all right! Dread cooled the blood pounding through Dylan's veins. Had he made a mistake coming back? Was Max going to frame him for Jilly's murder after all?

Panic subsided quickly and reason took over. Whether Dylan was in Canmore or not didn't matter. If Max had evidence that implicated him in Jilly's death, he would've handed it over to the RCMP already. He was just bluffing.

"You're full of bullshit, old man." He let Cathleen push him into the open passenger seat, but inside he seethed. Aware that two small faces peered out a front window, he slammed the door shut without any more fuss.

Strongman watched, a self-satisfied smile stretching lines on his sun-weathered face. He had plans up his sleeve, Dylan was certain of it. Beside him, Danny Mizzoni's shoulders were slumped, his head bowed submissively. There was something strange going on between those two, as well.

Dust was billowing behind their tires now. Dylan fixed his gaze ahead. "We've got our work cut out for us, darlin'."

"And then some," Cathleen agreed. "That man is as slimy and parasitic as a leech. Shut the window, Dylan. I feel like driving *fast*."

CHAPTER FIVE

THE TRANS-CANADA HIGHWAY connecting Canmore to Calgary permitted a speed of 110 kilometers an hour. Cathleen upped that another fifteen clicks, and still the tension from their meeting with Max Strongman clung.

He certainly wouldn't get her vote if he decided to run again for mayor in two years. Not that he'd gotten it the first time. Part of her wished Dylan had laid into him. But she didn't think that would've helped his cause with the townspeople. And if he had socked the mayor, word would definitely have traveled quickly.

As the roller-coaster outline from Calaway Park came into view, signaling the approaching city, Cathleen thought about the upcoming visit with her elder sister. On the phone, Maureen had been typically uncommunicative about her private life. Maybe because she was the oldest, she rarely burdened her sisters with her problems.

Cathleen glanced at Dylan. He was leaning back, his eyes almost but not quite, closed. Catching her glance, he grinned.

"Cooled down yet?"

"Some." She eased up on the speed a little. "Dylan, did you hear about Maureen's husband?"

The lines bracketing Dylan's mouth tightened. "Jake told me he was killed on a mountain in South America."

"Mount Aconcagua. According to the team he was climbing with, he took the ascent too quickly, even though the guides tried to get him to hold back. He died of altitude sickness."

"Damn fool. He never was one to listen to advice."

Cathleen knew Dylan hadn't liked Rod. She herself had never been that fond of her brother-in-law. Still... "You're one to talk about fools, Dylan. Riding wild bulls for the past two years!"

"Yeah, but I didn't have a wife and a kid."

Cathleen felt a flash of the old anger. "I get your point. It certainly wouldn't have mattered to me if you'd been killed by one of those crazy animals."

Now it was Dylan's turn to be quiet. After a minute, maybe two, he asked softly, "How are they doing? Maureen and Holly."

"Not good. Of course, it's only been four months...." Cathleen suspected her sister's grief was heavily laden with anger. Rod had always been searching for just one more adventure. Often he'd had close calls. But this time his luck had run out.

Now Rod was gone and Maureen was left to cope

with the aftermath. Or try to. Rod and Holly had been very close. Holly was lost without him. So far none of them, not even Maureen, had been able to reach the young girl in the depths of her grieving.

Cathleen stopped talking as traffic volumes increased. City driving wasn't her idea of fun. Her strategy was to drive a good five to ten kilometers faster than everyone else so she could weave around the slower drivers. She left the Number One Highway at Tenth Street, which took her across the Bow River. Navigating a series of turns to accommodate the one-way streets, she eventually ended up at the entrance of the parking lot opposite her sister's building on Seventh Avenue.

She stopped the Jeep with a lurch and cut the ignition. "We're here."

"Amazing." Dylan emerged from the other side of the Jeep, his step a little shaky. "Any chance you'll let me drive home?"

Cathleen dangled the keys in front of him before dropping them into the side pocket of her jacket. "Dream on, cowboy."

Leading the way across the paved parking lot, she jaywalked past two lanes reserved for light-rail transit, then climbed the stairs to the front doors of Elveden House. The building wasn't as impressive as the newer, taller office buildings in Calgary, with their sleek glass profiles, marble lobbies and bronzed glass elevators. But on the fifteenth floor, leasehold improvements financed by Maureen's legal firm were absolutely top-notch.

"Nice place," Dylan commented as they stepped off the elevator onto carpet so thick it almost swallowed their shoes.

Cathleen headed to the receptionist seated behind a curved granite desk. The young woman smiled as she continued to speak into a small mouthpiece attached to a set of headphones.

When she paused for a moment, Cathleen said quickly, "We're here to see Maureen Shannon."

The young woman nodded and waved them through a doorway to the right as she picked up another call. "Livingstone, Fagan and Shannon. How may I help you?"

Maureen waited outside her office door. Cathleen forced an immediate smile, to hide the jolt of shock she felt at seeing her sister so thin, tired and pale. Her silk suit had once fit like a second skin. Now it sagged. And her usually gorgeous blond hair was dull and shapeless.

"Good to see you, Maureen. You okay?" Cathleen hugged her sister's gaunt frame and wished she'd thought to bring along some of Poppy's fudge.

"We're hanging in." Though Maureen looked different, her voice sounded as confident and strong as ever. She pulled out of the embrace sooner than Cathleen was ready to let go and turned to Dylan.

Her hands planted on her hips, Maureen wasn't shy about giving him a careful once-over. "Never expected to see *you* again. Heard you were on the rodeo circuit in the States."

"Uh-huh. One of life's brief detours."

"Too bad you didn't *detour* by the church before you left. Do you know how often I've dreamed of planting my knee right in your—"

"Maureen!" Being the eldest was a responsibility her sister took seriously. "Go after him if you must, but keep your shots above the belt. You're a *mother* and respected *lawyer,* for heaven's sake."

Maureen laughed and allowed Cathleen to hook her arm around her waist. "God, I forget how much I miss you sometimes."

"Come visit more often, then that won't happen."

Abruptly, Maureen's expression became remote. She turned back to Dylan. "I guess we don't need to punch you. Looks like you've earned a few scars on your own."

"Not to mention a bum shoulder," he agreed. "Nothing a soak in the hot tub in Cathleen's backyard and a good massage wouldn't cure," he continued, winking at Cathleen.

"Fat chance. Better try physiotherapy sessions, cowboy."

Maureen watched the exchange, then shook her head. "Come on in, kids. I've got paying clients waiting for my time." She stepped aside for them to enter her office, then closed the door.

Cathleen went to her favorite leather chair, leaving the long sofa for Maureen and Dylan. Holly's picture on the desk haunted her. Big smile, glowing eyes. Poor kid. Her father's death surely marked the end of innocent childhood happiness for Holly.

"I have a lunch meeting, so I'll make this quick." Maureen grabbed a small notebook from her desk. "Cathleen said you wanted information about your stepfather. You're aware he was married before?"

Dylan nodded.

"His ex-wife still lives in Calgary. I have her name and current address...." She handed Dylan a rectangular card.

"Maureen, you're a peach." Dylan slipped the card into the front pocket of his denim shirt.

His compliment didn't faze Maureen. "You'll note the address isn't in the best part of town. Presumably she could've used a better lawyer in the divorce proceedings."

"Maybe she considered getting rid of Max bonus enough," Dylan said. "Has Cathleen told you what we think is going on with Max and my mother?"

"Yes and I'm sorry. These situations can be very tricky."

"No kidding. I'm looking for something—anything—that might jolt Mom into facing reality. So anything we can find out about Max..."

"Well, it was easy enough for me to dig up the basics. One of my partners knew him back in the days when he worked in the oil patch here in Calgary. Max grew up and went to school in the city, too. He relocated to Edmonton for university, and after graduation took a job at Shell, then moved to one of the smaller local firms. Here's something interesting." Maureen flipped the page of her notebook. "For one of his oil projects, Max spent several months in Canmore. That would have been over twenty years ago. Curious that he ended up there once more when he married your mother."

"He moved back before he married my mother," Dylan corrected her. "He'd started a property development company and had gone out to the ranch to talk about buying her land."

Cathleen knew how much Dylan rued that day. If only he'd been home and his mother away, how differently their lives would've turned out.

After a worried glance at Cathleen, Maureen asked, "What about this Jilly Beckett matter? Kelly and I are concerned, as you can imagine."

Dylan opened his hands as if to indicate he had nothing to hide. "That was Max's doing. I have no idea how I'm going to prove it, though."

"I've kept up-to-date on the case. The Becketts live in our neighborhood, and Jilly's death has almost destroyed them both. Almost immediately after the shooting, Conrad Beckett retired from the board of Beckett Oil and Gas and sold most of his shares to one of the large petroleum conglomerates in the States.''

Cathleen remembered reading about the resignation in the business section of the Calgary paper. At the time she'd been struck by the futility of it all. Conrad had devoted his life to building that company for his daughter. With her gone, no wonder he lost interest.

''I've always thought an arrest and subsequent conviction would do much to ease Conrad and Linda's pain,'' Maureen continued. ''But as I understand it, the evidence, such as it is, is purely circumstantial.''

''Don't I know it.''

Maureen was silent for a few minutes, taking Dylan's measure. ''I have to admit it doesn't make me happy to have Cathleen involved in this.''

''Don't talk about me like I'm not in the room. And for God's sake, stop worrying.'' It was plain to Cathleen that her sister, not her, was the one they should all be concerned about.

Maureen shrugged. ''There never was any telling you what to do.''

That sure never stopped you from trying. Cathleen held back the somewhat unfair words. As the eldest sister, Maureen had often been left in charge of her younger siblings. It was only natural she took on the role of surrogate mother occasionally.

"Thanks for the help," Dylan said.

"I wish you would come visit us soon," Cathleen added.

"I will." Maureen glanced at the photo of her daughter as she spoke.

"By the way," Dylan added when they were almost out the door. "My cousin Jake said to say hello."

"Oh?" For the first time, a little natural color stained Maureen's cheekbones. "I'm surprised he remembers me. We only met at your engagement party."

"Now, those were happier days," he said.

"Sometimes I wonder," Maureen replied.

USING THE INFORMATION on the back of the card Maureen had given him, supplemented by a dog-eared map of Calgary he found stashed under the passenger seat of Cathleen's Jeep, Dylan navigated to the home of Max Strongman's first wife. Cathleen did her best to make good time, racing for every green light and impatiently passing the slower drivers.

"Have you been talking to Jake in Australia?" she asked.

He shook his head. "Nah. I kind of made that last bit up. I've always wondered if Jake had a thing for Maureen. Did you notice him watching her at our engagement party?''

''But Maureen's husband was there!''

''I never said he did anything but watch, did I?'' He squinted at an approaching street sign. ''Take that left.''

Tanya Strongman—apparently she hadn't changed her name after dissolving her marriage—lived in the basement of a small house in Inglewood. The area, close to the Bow River and to downtown, was becoming trendy with urbanites. But Tanya's house was definitely not in the fashionable section. Its location close to the highway where Blackfoot Trail met Ninth Avenue, brought the noise and exhaust of the big trucks traveling back and forth from the industrial district.

Dylan was relieved when they found the middle-aged woman at home. She opened her door about ten centimeters and peered up at them. The petite woman's faded beauty was reminiscent of his mother's in happier years. Dylan introduced himself, then Cathleen. Though obviously puzzled, Tanya relented enough to ease the door open farther.

''What do you want?''

''We're sorry to disturb you,'' he said, ''but we were hoping you could give us some information about Max Strongman.'' When Tanya didn't reply, he added, ''He *was* your ex-husband?''

"How do you know Max?" She glanced furtively toward the street, as if afraid of who might be out there.

"My mother married him."

"Oh." Her expression shifted, became sharper and yet somehow warmer, too. "You poor thing." She pushed the door out in a wide, welcoming arc. "Come on in."

During the next half hour, Tanya told the story of her first and only marriage. Max had been controlling and prone to jealousy at first.

"He hated me talking to other men. Which was ironic, because while I remained completely faithful to him, I'm certain he cheated on me at least once during our marriage. That was hard to take, but it wasn't until he started getting physically violent that our life became really unbearable."

"And when was that?"

"Shortly after James started school and I found a part-time job. The first time Max hit me it was just a slap to the face. For the sake of our family, I gave him a second chance, and for several years he was pretty good. But on our tenth anniversary, we went out for dinner. When we came home, he went berserk. And all because of a compliment one of the waiters gave me. James and I spent that night in the Calgary Women's Shelter. The next day, Max found me there and begged me to come back. Even though I was afraid, I stuck to my guns. I had a lot of support, but I didn't feel truly safe until I heard he'd moved to Canmore and remarried. I'm sorry my gain was your mother's loss.''

''How wise you were to leave the marriage,'' Cathleen said.

''That's what everyone says. But there are times when I question whether it was worth it. After the divorce I struggled for years with emotional problems that made it very difficult for me to hold a job. During those hard times, he took my son away from me. Now I have a job, but it pays barely more than minimum wage.''

Her gaze bounced around the four walls of her shabby kitchen. ''When I was with Max, I had a beautiful home and my child. Now...''

Cathleen had been leaning progressively closer to Tanya as she spoke. She reached for the other woman's hand. ''Do you ever see James anymore?''

Stark grief highlighted the lines in Tanya's face. ''No. I had visitation rights when he was younger, but Max has convinced him I'm a flake. My son hasn't come to visit since he was eighteen. He won't answer my phone calls or my letters. I'm afraid Max has always had a hold over him. The poor child wanted so desperately to please his father, but Max made that very, very difficult.''

Dylan rubbed his forehead. Tanya's tale brought him an almost physical pain. Max Strongman, it appeared, specialized in coming between the women he married and their children. Poor James. It sounded as though he'd had it rough from the very beginning.

"That is so sad," Cathleen said finally. "I wish we could help you."

One side of Tanya's mouth lifted in an attempted smile. "It's too late for us, I'm afraid. But maybe it's not too late for your mother." She patted Dylan on the knee.

"I'd do anything to help her get away from him."

Tanya frowned. "I'm sure you would. But it won't be easy unless she's ready to ask for your assistance."

"Not so far," Dylan said. "My mother is determined to stand by the bastard."

"Then there's probably nothing you can do."

Dylan's smile was grim. "Not the answer I was looking for."

"Forgive me for not being more positive. I lived with the man for ten years. When he wants something, it's just about impossible to stop him."

DYLAN AND CATHLEEN PULLED into a café after their visit with Tanya Strongman. Cathleen wasn't very hungry, so she ordered a salad—a choice she regretted when Dylan's hot beef sandwich and fries were delivered ten minutes later.

"How come I didn't see it sooner?" Dylan asked. He dipped one end of his sandwich into a small bowl of sauce.

Cathleen tried to comfort him. "Maybe it hasn't been as bad for your mother as it was for Tanya." She thought of the bruises on Rose's leg. "Or maybe at least it wasn't in the beginning. The big change in your mother didn't occur until after Jilly Beckett's death...." *And Dylan's disappearance.*

Dylan didn't need long to make the same connection. "God, I left her alone with that bastard...."

Cathleen grasped one of his hands. "What about Rose's friends, including me? None of us noticed. Not one of us has helped her. The really frustrating thing is that it sounds like there's nothing we *can* do to help."

He turned his hand so he was now holding hers. "Like Tanya said, Mom has to be ready to help herself."

"Maybe. Maybe not."

"What do you mean?"

"Dylan, if we *could* nail Max with Jilly's death, he'd end up in jail. Your name would be cleared and your mother would be free. It would be the perfect solution...."

"Absolutely correct, darlin'."

She felt silly then, realizing that this was, after all, the reason Dylan had come back. To nail Max.

And now she'd just bought into the entire scheme. Outmaneuvered once more, and so subtly she still wasn't sure how it had happened....

Finished with her salad, she inspected Dylan's lunch. "By the way, if you're not eating the fries, can I have them?"

BEFORE HEADING BACK to Canmore, Cathleen drove to the Mount Royal address that Dylan still remembered. The contrast from the Inglewood neighborhood couldn't have been greater. Here were estate homes, beautiful landscaping, gracious living for Calgary's wealthiest.

Cathleen parked across from the Becketts' house, mere blocks from Maureen's, and killed the ignition.

"They had a TV crew out here two years ago, just hours after it happened," Dylan told her. "Interviewing neighbors, taking shots of the house where Jilly had grown up. I remember that was her bedroom window."

He pointed to the shuttered glass pane on the far right of the second story of the Tudor-style home. Cathleen got out of the Jeep and leaned against the door.

"Remember what it was like to be sixteen, Dylan?"

"I sure do." He came round the Jeep to stand beside her, taking her hand.

It was the third time they'd touched that day.

"I heard she was a top student. Planning to take business in university before following in her daddy's footsteps."

Beckett Oil and Gas had been a true Calgary success story. Despite volatile ups and downs in the resource market, the multimillion-dollar public company had remained family-controlled through to the new millennium, surviving several hostile takeover bids. What a shame that it was gone now, devoured by a multibillion-dollar corporation in the wake of Conrad Beckett's resignation.

Dylan nodded. "That's why Jilly was out at the ranch that day. She'd been working all summer with her father. Conrad wanted her in on the final decision. They didn't count on our protest interrupting the proceedings."

The grinding noise of the Becketts' garage opener startled them both into silence. Smoothly the paneled door lifted, just in time to receive a silver Mercedes four-door, with a woman at the wheel.

This had to be Jilly Beckett's mother, Linda. In one glance, Cathleen noticed expensively coiffed hair and a pair of concealing sunglasses. No one else was in the car.

Dylan seemed transfixed by the woman's unexpected appearance and continued to stare, even after the stained wood door had slid back into place.

"Are you okay, Dylan?"

"I think we should knock on the front door and ask to talk to her."

"Why?" She'd already been questioning his motives for stopping by in the first place. Memories of that day had to be so painful for him.

"I've always wondered what her husband saw. Jilly was standing right beside him."

Linda Beckett must have come out from a side door, then approached them from behind the thick lilac hedge that bordered one side of her property. Because suddenly she was there, nodding.

"Yes. Conrad caught Jilly in his arms after she was shot. It's a small comfort to me that he was with her when it happened. But unfortunately he didn't see who was responsible."

Linda held herself tall, but her head trembled slightly as she spoke. When she held out her hand, it, too, contained a trace of a tremor. Nerves? Cathleen wondered.

"You may not want to shake my hand, ma'am," Dylan said. "Some people blame me for what happened to your daughter."

"I know who you are, Dylan McLean. I know everyone who was present that day at the ranch. But you—" She slipped off her sunglasses and tucked them into her purse as she turned to Cathleen. "I've not had the pleasure."

"Cathleen Shannon, Mrs. Beckett." Cathleen

toned down her usual firm handshake. Mrs. Beckett's hand felt as fragile and cold as fine bone china.

"You weren't there."

"No."

"Jilly was our only child."

As Mrs. Beckett began walking toward the house, it seemed natural to follow her. A flagstone path led to three shallow stairs and an arched oak door.

"I think of her often," Dylan said. "We were on opposite sides on this particular issue, but I could tell she was a real bright kid, with a great future ahead of her."

"There was no curbing her ambition. I tried to get her to slow down, to have a little fun. But all she ever wanted was to work with her daddy. Would you like to see her room?"

Cathleen exchanged a glance with Dylan, and he nodded slightly. It would have been heartless to say no. Gleaming oak stairs led up from the spacious foyer. At the landing, Mrs. Beckett turned right, toward the window Dylan had pointed out earlier. For the second time that day, Cathleen's boots were lost in plush carpeting.

Mrs. Beckett opened a set of double doors, revealing a spacious suite. The rooms were decorated in denim and yellow, and it was clear that besides her daddy's business, Jilly had had at least one other passion in her life. Horses.

Pictures of the animals, most of them quarter horses, adorned the walls, and on the top of the bookshelf was an impressive china collection of several North American breeds. At the foot of her bed stood an old wooden rocking horse that must have been saved from when she was a toddler. Dylan ran a hand over the worn seat, and Cathleen knew just how he felt. The hurt was a heaviness everyone who'd known Jilly would carry all their lives. Especially her parents.

Jilly's mother sank into a chair against the wall. Cathleen got the impression she spent a lot of time sitting there.

"I miss her so much." Linda Beckett's mouth trembled. "I wonder if she had a moment when she realized what was happening. The doctors told me death would've been instantaneous. But I can't believe there wasn't a split second of fear."

Cathleen moved to the vanity table set up by the window. Lip glosses, eye shadow, hair gel and glitter body lotion. At Jilly's age, a whole new world had been opening. A world she would now never know. It was so unfair.

"All we've cared about since the…since she was shot…is that justice be served. We want that killer to pay for what happened to our baby. Somehow—" she turned to Dylan "—we've never thought that person was you. Angry as he was at that demonstration, my husband felt you were an honorable man. And he's not often wrong about people.''

Dylan's cheeks reddened. Cathleen could guess how he felt. Of all the people to finally speak in his favor, it had to be the victim's mother.

''What does your husband think about Max Strongman?'' Cathleen asked.

''That,'' replied Mrs. Beckett, ''is a completely different matter. Conrad never trusted him. If he hadn't retired from Beckett Oil and Gas, those oil wells on the Bar M would never have been drilled.''

CHAPTER SIX

ONE DAY IN THE CITY was enough for Dylan. Back at Larch Lodge he went out to the barn to pay his respects to Cascade. He'd named her after the mountain he and Cathleen had been climbing the first time they made love, but remembering that day was a bittersweet pleasure now.

He fixed the sticky barn door, then busied himself with a few more chores. The familiar work made him hunger for the life he'd been born to, the rancher's life. It killed him knowing that just a stone's throw from here his land sat idle and uncared for.

Afterward he took a shower, then checked in the kitchen. Dinner was long over, and the dishes had been cleaned. He made himself a sandwich, ate in solitude, then cased out the adjoining dining and living rooms. No sign of life. Had everyone gone to bed?

Prowling past the staircase and down the hall, he found Cathleen in the study. A pale beam of light spilled from the partially open door into the hall. He eased the door wider. Cathleen sat at her desk, her head bent low so that all he could see was her hair. It hung almost to the desktop, waves of dark brown streaked with chestnut, glowing in the light from the halogen desk lamp.

A steady heat emanated from the fireplace, the sound system played familiar tunes from the country music station in Calgary and a bottle of brandy stood open on her desk, a snifter beside it. A cozy domestic scene...

"Damn bloody stupid numbers!"

He smiled. Must be working on the account books. She'd always hated math. According to their original plans, made a million years ago, that was to have been his job. He winced a little at the thought of what was to have been, what *should* have been.

Could he have stayed and married her two years ago? With hindsight he knew running away had been a fool's solution. But going ahead with the wedding would've been just as unwise, regardless of how much Cathleen said she believed in him. His mother had been right on that point. Cathleen deserved more than a suspected criminal for her husband.

He moved forward, into her line of vision. "Nice to hear you cursing at something other than me for a change."

Her head jerked up. "Damn it, Dylan. Trying to

give me a heart attack? I thought you'd gone to bed by now. And what the hell are you wearing?''

He ignored the question, since the answer was obvious. After his shower he'd slipped on the white terry robe hanging on the back of his bedroom door. Provided by management. The same management now focusing on the gap at the front of the robe where the two sides crossed over on his chest. Cathleen's gaze slid downward and he knew she was thinking he wouldn't be wearing anything underneath. She was right.

''Figured I'd see if that hot tub might help my sore arm. Now that I'm an official lodge guest and all.''

He strolled to the cabinet where she kept her supplies and picked out a glass. Helping himself to her brandy, he poured an inch into his snifter and another inch into hers. Then he headed to the fireplace, where the intense heat almost singed the cotton of his robe.

Cathleen leaned back in her chair, settling her feet on a metal filing cabinet next to the desk. He eyed her red boots appreciatively. Like everything else about her, from her tousled hair to her generous curved lips, they were sexy as hell.

He pulled one of the leather chairs closer to her and sat.

''What about the hot tub?''

"I'm in no hurry." He glanced at the papers on her desk. "Everything balancing out okay?"

"No, everything is not balancing out okay." She swung one leg over and pushed at the account books with the heel of her boot. "Damn numbers never cooperate."

"Want me to take a look in the morning?"

"No, I don't. What's with you? Fixing the door in the barn, now offering to do the bookkeeping..."

"Just trying to make myself indispensable."

"Hah! If *you* were indispensable, where would *I* be now?"

Ow. The lady was sharp. "Are we never going to move past that? I apologized, didn't I?"

She let her legs fall with a thud to the floor. "I suppose you figure that makes us square."

"Well, why not? Cath, I made a mistake. But I came back, right? And I'm here now...." He rubbed his hands over the soft worn leather on the arms of the chair. Cathleen's boots would feel rougher, he decided. But if they were to make love, he still wouldn't want her to take them off....

"Dylan, don't look at me like that."

He had to grin. He was willing to bet their thoughts had been traveling in the same direction. That was to his advantage, and was probably his only one. "Darlin', there is no other way for me to look at you."

"You're insufferable, you know that? Don't you ever give up?"

"No, and someday you're going to be glad about that."

"Oh, you think so?"

"I do." The words seemed to hang in the air several seconds after he said them, reminding him of wedding vows not spoken. He cleared his throat and abandoned his chair. "Ready for the hot tub?"

Once more her gaze dropped to the opening of his robe. "I don't think so...."

"Oh, come on. You deserve a break. I'll sort those books out in the morning." He turned off her desk lamp, then moved behind her chair. Holding his brandy glass in one hand, he curled the other around her neck and felt for the muscles that led to her shoulders. Hard, tensed muscles. "Ease up, darlin'. You've got more knots than the rope on that last bull I rode before I packed up for home."

"He must've been a bruiser." She tipped her head back, easing into the massage.

"Almost two thousand pounds, but as agile as a steer. I managed to last my eight seconds and earn my prize money, before he left me with his parting memento."

Her voice shifted to a lower, gentler note. "What happened?"

"The outriders came up from my left after the buzzer. Just as I was preparing to jump, that wily old bull started spinning to the right. I flew off like a novice, and the bull gunned for me.''

''Did he gouge your shoulder?''

''Nah. Stepped on it.'' It had hurt and still did. But Dylan couldn't regret the accident. He'd needed something drastic to make him realize his new lifestyle wasn't working. Traveling from rodeo to rodeo, surviving one adrenaline-charged moment to the next, couldn't make him forget what he'd left behind.

Dylan leaned down a little, to catch the scent from her hair. Some kind of botanical shampoo with herbs and grasses and stuff. Or maybe it was just the smell of the pasture carried in by the wind from the partially open door.

''Darlin', do you have a white bathrobe hanging on your door, too?''

Her back straightened; her muscles stiffened. ''Dylan, I am not getting into that hot tub with you. Do you think I don't know what you've got on under that robe?''

''So?'' He bent lower, tracing the soft curve of her ear with his lips. ''Why don't you wear the same thing? And bring your brandy. It's a clear night. The stars will be incredible.''

Not that *he* cared. If Cathleen was with him, he'd be looking at nothing but her. It amazed him how hungry he still was for the sight of her, the sound of her voice, the slightest touch between them.

Slowly he set down his glass, so he could use both of his hands, turning his massage into a caress. He ran his fingers past her shoulders and down her arms. Nuzzling the side of her head, he was sure he could feel her relenting.

Please, Cath, please. Give me a chance....

"Go to hell, Dylan." The words came out husky, but her meaning was clear. She shifted out of his arms and switched on her desk lamp once more.

Disappointment burned, but he couldn't let her see it. His confidence, his constancy, would win her over in the end. He had to believe that or go insane.

"I guess you're scared, right? Afraid you won't be able to resist me if you get too close."

"Face it, Dylan. I'd rather spend my night with an account book. That ought to tell you something."

"That you're a masochist?"

She tossed her pen at him. "Get out of here!"

He caught the ballpoint and set it carefully on her desk. "You better stop saying things like that, or one day I'll take you at your word. *Then* you'll really be sorry...."

Dylan went to stand by the patio doors, facing out toward the hot tub, but he didn't leave. Quietly Cathleen slipped her checkbook into the top drawer of her desk. She couldn't focus on debits and credits during the best of times. It was impossible when Dylan had seduction on his agenda. From day one of his showing up at her B and B she'd set the parameters of their involvement, and from day one he'd continued to ignore them.

Right now she felt like throwing the darn account books at his back, but it was really herself she was mad at. Why did she still want him so badly? She knew the charm was all surface, and yet every time he smiled at her, her toes curled into the hard leather soles of her boots. And every time his eyes promised her it was inevitable that they become lovers again, she found herself hoping it could be true.

Yet that was impossible. The sex was tempting, but it came with a hefty price tag, and she was neither weak nor foolish enough to make that mistake again.

Brave words, Cathleen realized. But could she live by them? Dylan was right. She *was* afraid to put herself to the test. Today there'd been so many instances when she'd wanted to hug him, hold him close, kiss him. Alone in the hot tub, *naked* in the hot tub, how would she resist?

The safest thing would be to go to bed this instant. She switched off her desk lamp, leaving only the golden glow from the fireplace. Dylan tensed, but didn't turn.

Now was the perfect opportunity to slip away.... Instead, she drifted over to the patio doors. Separating the slats on the blinds, she peered out at the covered hot tub.

"Changed your mind?" Dylan asked.

"Not likely." She was close enough for him to touch, and felt disappointed when he didn't even try. *Say good-night and leave.* She knew it was the smart thing to do, but didn't.

She reached for the lapel of his robe, and eased it off his shoulder. With solemn gray eyes he watched her closely, but made no move to stop her. When she'd revealed his scar—a long gash of puckered pink skin—she stopped.

"Pretty ugly, huh?"

"Yeah. Pretty ugly." She felt compelled to touch it, but the moment her fingers came into contact with his skin, Dylan sucked in his breath.

She jerked her hand away. "Does it hurt?"

"For a second there, it didn't." In fact, he half expected that the next time he checked in the mirror, the red puckered skin would be smooth and healed.

"I'm sorry," she said, but he had no idea what she was apologizing for. Touching him? Withdrawing? Or, more likely, that he'd been injured in the first place?

"I'm glad it happened," he said. "Or I might not be here."

She turned her face toward the window again. "Was it hard to come back?"

"Harder than I thought." Not that he cared about the treatment he'd received in Canmore. Cathleen's opinion was the one that counted. And his mother's. Yet on both scores he'd been disappointed, for different reasons.

"You don't have to stay."

"Hey, I've prepaid for the month." She didn't smile. Did that mean that already she regretted letting him take one of her rooms? That instead of making progress with her, he was actually falling behind?

"Ever think about the good times, Cath?"

"Truth?"

He felt as if his heart had stopped, but he nodded.

"I try not to."

That hurt. He'd filled the years he'd been away with memories of her. Their best times together had gotten him through his worst times alone.

"That's an awful lot of years to block out."

"I know it." She raised her eyes, and for one awful second he saw such sadness it choked the breath out of him.

"Oh, darlin'..." He'd hurt her so badly; he'd never realized how badly. She really must've loved him...once.

"We had something extraordinary," she said softly.

"Yes." Together they'd been wild, crazy, young

and in love. They'd shared friendship, compatibil-
ity, dynamite sex....

"But it's gone, Dylan. Even if I wanted to, I
couldn't feel about you the way I once did."

If she'd spoken with bitter anger, he might have
been able to stand it. But her calm, almost overly
rational words burned like acid. She reached out a
hand, and her fingers landed on his scar again. She
traced it gently with her healing touch, as if she
could make up for her wounding words.

"That doesn't matter," he said desperately. "We
belong together. It doesn't have to be the same."

She shook her head. "How could we accept anything less? That's the worst of it, Dylan. You
spoiled me for anything less."

Suddenly she was turning, moving away from
him.

"Where are you going?"

She ignored his outstretched hand. "I'm tired.
Go ahead and have your soak. I'll see you in the
morning."

He didn't want a soak. He wanted only her. But
she was already gone, out the door. He let his head
drop to the cool glass of the patio door and blinked
away a strange, moist feeling in his eyes.

He'd been wrong, so wrong, in all his calcula-
tions. Wrong to leave, wrong to come back. Wrong
to think that once he was here, once he and Cathleen were together...

Illusions and false hope had kept him going for the past two years. Now that both had been shattered, what did that leave him for the future? The answer, he was afraid, was all too little.

CHAPTER SEVEN

DYLAN HADN'T SLEPT ALL NIGHT, so it wasn't right to say he awoke at dawn. But that was when he threw back his covers and got out of bed. Brushing a hand through his hair, he yawned and strode to the window.

The grass outside glistened as if it had been silver plated. The dew had frozen, and he wondered how much the temperature had dropped. It felt like below freezing here in his room. He stepped into clean underwear and jeans, then layered his warmest flannel shirt over a plain white T-shirt.

He almost headed for the door, then remembered he really had no place to go and nothing much to do. No horses to feed, no cattle to water, no fences to mend.

So he went back to the window. He angled himself to get the best view of Thunder Valley, the land his family had ranched ever since they'd come out west in the early eighteen hundreds. His need to be out on that land, riding a horse and feeling the cold autumn wind brushing over his cheeks, was so strong it hurt.

Maybe he should look into another temporary job, just to get himself back on a horse and feeling useful. But who would hire him the way things stood? If he wanted a job, he'd have to move on. And he couldn't do that yet.

This time, it wasn't about Cathleen. After last night, he was finally convinced that nothing he said or did was ever going to convince her to love him again. He could prove he was innocent—hell, he could get himself voted Citizen of the Year—and she wouldn't care. She'd been saying it from the start, but last night he'd finally believed her.

If it wasn't for his mother, he'd have packed up and been gone before morning. On the off chance that he still might be able to do something to help Rose, though, he'd chosen to stay.

A sound from the hallway told him he was no longer the only one out of bed. He listened to the bathroom door open and sat down to wait. If it was Cathleen, he didn't want to see her. Not yet. One look at his face and she'd know how much he'd suffered. Maybe it was petty, but he didn't want to give her the satisfaction.

"DID YOU CUT YOURSELF shaving?" Poppy asked as she slid the western omelet onto his plate.

"Once or twice." He'd removed the bits of tissue before coming down to take a look at the accounts, but the red marks remained. Score yet another point for Cathleen. His hand was usually as steady as a farrier's.

He scooped a forkful of eggs into his mouth, then glanced around the kitchen. Poppy had been busy. He'd heard the clattering while he was matching receipts to entries, quickly discovering a transposition error that explained why Cathleen had been unable to balance last night. Now he saw a batch of bread dough, covered by a blue-checked cloth, sitting in a sunny spot on the counter to rise.

"Baking again, Poppy?"

"Just plain old cinnamon buns."

"Cathleen will be happy. They're her favorite." Or at least, they had been. Perhaps she had a different favorite now. Like banana bread. Maybe she'd crossed cinnamon buns off her list the way she'd crossed *him* off.

Oh, stop your sulking. She'd been better to him than he'd had any right to ask. She'd let him stay in her house—something he doubted anyone else in Canmore, except Jake, would have allowed.

And she'd been generous with her time and effort in trying to help his mother and in trying to help *him.* She'd been honest from the start about the chances of a reconciliation. Nil.

So he had no right to feel angry or resentful. Even though everything he'd done, he'd done for her. Did she think he'd *wanted* to clear off on their wedding day? He'd had no choice. How could he stay and expect her to honor a commitment she'd made when he'd been a successful rancher, heir to three thousand acres of land and not a penniless cowboy who also happened to be a suspected murderer.

Old ground, buddy. Stop spinning your wheels. You've apologized and she wouldn't accept it. You tried to seduce her and she turned the tables on you. Face it, you gambled and lost.

The screen door banged open, and Kip bounded in.

"Hey there, boy." Dylan slipped him a piece of sausage, then scratched under his collar. Cathleen came in right behind her dog. He watched her hang her hat on one of the pegs on the wall.

She looked wonderful. Obviously she hadn't tossed and turned last night. Or maybe it was just the hour out on her horse that had given her skin that high color, her dark eyes a glow.

"What a great run. The barn door glides with the lightest touch. Thanks, Dylan." She spied the bowl in the corner. "Don't tell me you're baking again, Poppy, as well as making us all breakfast. Although I must admit I'm starving."

She held out her plate, and Poppy inverted a perfectly cooked omelet from the frying pan. His gut tightened as Cathleen added several sausages and helped herself to a tall glass of juice.

He resented her appetite because it told him he

was the only one feeling sick after last night. *I'm happy and healthy and I don't need you.* Each forkful of food that made its way to her mouth and down to her stomach proved the same damn thing.

He couldn't handle food, but coffee was another story. Dylan grabbed the handle of his mug and took a long swallow. A good caffeine buzz might make it possible to smile. Eventually.

"Did you sleep well?" he finally asked.

"Sure did. And you?"

"Oh yeah, great," he lied. "Would've stayed in bed longer, but someone was making all this racket in the kitchen." He winked at Poppy so she'd know he was teasing.

In what seemed like no time, Cathleen's plate was empty. "Let me clean up these breakfast dishes, Poppy," she said, "so you can get back to your book. Make sure that omelet recipe gets included. It was delicious."

"It will. But I don't need to rush off. Plenty of time for writing later." Poppy got up from the table and began stacking dishes. Dylan tried to force down a few more mouthfuls so he wouldn't insult her cooking. The omelet *was* delicious, but who could eat with Cathleen flitting around like she was the happiest person on earth?

"What do you plan to do today?" Cathleen asked him.

"Thought I'd make some phone calls about a

few trucks I saw for sale in yesterday's paper.''
Having no means of transportation was wearing
thin. At first, depending on Cathleen to get around
had seemed a good way to force her to spend time
with him. But look how well that strategy had
panned out.

The kitchen phone rang, and as Cathleen moved
to answer it, Dylan used the distraction to scrape
his leftovers into the garbage. He'd loaded his
dishes in the dishwasher and was heading for the
newspaper with his second cup of coffee when
Cathleen called him.

''Dylan, that was your mother. She wants you to
stop by for a drink this evening. Around eight
o'clock.''

He froze. ''You're sure?''

Cathleen nodded, her expression sober. ''I asked
if she wanted to talk to you now, but she said to
just pass on the message.''

For a moment they stared at each other. In Cathleen's eyes, Dylan felt he could read all his own
desperate hopes. That she wanted to see him had to
be a good sign. Maybe she was ready to repair the
bond between them. And maybe, just maybe, this
might turn out to be the first step that would free
her from Max Strongman.

AT 7:45 THAT EVENING, Dylan drove his own truck
into Canmore. He'd purchased it that afternoon,

secondhand from a woman who'd decided the suspension was a little stiff for her taste. It felt perfect to him. He was glad to have his own wheels and independence once more.

In Canmore, he parked in front of his mother's house on Grassi Place. The sun had set a while ago, and he could see a light on in one of the front rooms on the main floor. How would she be tonight? He hoped to God this was going to be a turning point in their relationship.

He ran up the walk, remembering the first time he'd been here, with Cathleen. This time when he rang the bell, however, his mother answered right away.

"Come in, Dylan."

She was wearing some kind of lounging outfit. The gray silk appeared pricey, but it didn't do her complexion any good. She appeared even older than the last time he'd seen her.

"Are you okay?"

"Of course I am." She stared at him a moment, her emotions obviously at war. Finally she sighed and stepped back into the house. "Would you like a drink?"

She led him into a room off to the left. One of the colorless formal rooms he'd avoided on his last visit. Two leather sofas faced each other, at right angles to a white stucco fireplace. She headed for a tall cabinet against the wall.

"Rye and soda? Your father always drank rye and soda."

"Sure." He didn't sit down but followed her. She had ice ready, in a bucket, and he used a pair of silver tongs to pick out a cube for each of them. She poured both the rye and the soda with trembling hands.

"Since Max is out this evening, I thought it would be a good chance for us to talk."

"Yes?" He waited as she settled herself on one of the sofas, then sat directly opposite her, leaning over his legs so he could really study her. Since he'd arrived, she'd avoided looking straight at him. That made him uneasy. He decided to take the conversation in his own hands for a minute.

"Cathleen and I went to Calgary yesterday. We looked up a few people, including Max's first wife."

"Oh, Dylan. Why would you do that?"

"I figured it was time I checked into the man you married. Mom, I only wish I'd done it sooner."

She pressed the fingers of one hand against her temple, and he remembered Tanya's advice. *She won't believe you. Not unless she's ready…*

Well, maybe his mother was ready. After all, she'd asked to see him. "Max pulled the same stuff with his first wife that he's pulling with you. He tried to control her, and when she wouldn't do exactly as he said, he hit her. It didn't stop until she left him.''

He could tell by his mother's expression that his words weren't penetrating.

''You've got it all wrong. Max told me you'd say that. Tanya lied to you, son. Max's first wife is a crazy, unstable woman. When James was only ten, Max had to take full custody because she wasn't capable of looking after the poor boy.''

''Did you ever wonder what made Tanya Strongman so unstable?''

''Oh, Dylan. You've always been so quick to judge. Can't you believe Max really loves me? And he needs me. In some ways, even more than your father did.''

''Don't compare my father with that man.'' In no way did Bud McLean come short next to Max Strongman.

''That's why you've never been able to warm up to Max. For you, no one could ever measure up to your father. But I was too young to spend the rest of my life alone.''

Every word she said made sense. He knew it was true. He *had* idolized his father. No matter what man his mother had remarried, there would've been problems. But she was just skirting the main issue here. ''If Max loves you so much, why aren't you happy?''

''Why do you think I'm not happy?''

"Look at yourself, for God's sake! Mom, you must see the changes when you're in front of the mirror. Why don't you belong to the horticultural society anymore? Why don't any of your old friends visit like they used to? And don't pin it on me this time. Even if I was the criminal your husband claims I am, no one would blame you."

"I've not been well...." Rose had polished off her drink and was about to make herself another one. He took the glass and did it for her, going easy on the liquor.

"Are you sick, Mom? What does Dr. Rutherford say?" He passed her the glass but was too concerned to sit. Instead, he paced to the fireplace, where the smooth mantel contained nothing but a crystal vase with some sort of modern, silk flower arrangement. His mother's favorite flowers for the fall were chrysanthemums. Why didn't she have any of those in this vase?

"I don't go to Dr. Rutherford anymore. Max takes me to Calgary, to the specialists there. You see, that's how much he loves me. He's always insisted on only the best. My clothing, this house, our vehicle..."

"Yeah, and all paid for with *your* money. Answer me this. How does he treat you? Does he ever hit you?"

His mother peered into her glass, as if searching

for something she'd dropped. From outside, Dylan heard the muffled sound of barking.

"Max isn't perfect, but he's my husband," Rose said. "I called you here because there's something important I have to tell you."

"What is it, Ma?"

The white cat slipped between his legs, brushing against his jeans. Maybe she'd heard the distant dog and was frightened. He reached out a hand, but she eluded him, turning instead to his mother, who picked her up and placed her in the hollow of her lap.

"Come here, precious."

Something in his mother's voice struck a chord. Hadn't she taken that tone with him, once upon a time, back when he was very little?

"I want you to do something for me," Rose said, her voice firmer now.

"Of course I will. Whatever you want." He took a few steps closer, hoping…

"You've made a big mistake coming back to Canmore. Max has been very upset. And it's not fair to Cathleen, either. That girl needs to forget about you. And you…son, you need to find someplace to make a clean start."

Asking him to leave again; that was what this was about. Not some sentimental mother-son reunion. What a fool he was to have even hoped for anything else. The whole scenario reminded him of their last conversation two years ago. That time she hadn't actually asked him to leave Canmore, but she'd put some pretty plain words to him.

"How can you marry that lovely girl after what you've done? She'll be forced to leave her home. That or live under the shadow of your disgrace for the rest of her life..."

Dylan blinked. His mother was still speaking.

"If you ever loved me, Dylan, go and don't come back. I don't want you to visit me, or even call or write."

"So the ranch belongs to the Strongmans, then. Is that what you've decided?"

"Actually, no. Tomorrow I'm changing my will. I called my accountant. He's someone I trust. He's going to arrange for a lawyer to come by tomorrow. You and Jake will get the McLean land. But not until I'm gone."

Much as he needed that land, he sure as hell didn't want his mother to die in order for him to lay his claim. "I don't understand. If you're willing to do that much, why do you want me to leave?"

"I can't explain. Just go. Or I'll leave the will the way it is, with everything going to Max and James."

"Damn it! You're not being fair!"

She said nothing; instead she set the cat gently on the sofa and headed back to the cabinet.

He felt furious then—didn't she know she was

just hiding from her problems? "That's right, Mother. Have another drink. I'm sure that will help."

For a moment her hands stilled, then she resumed pouring the liquor into her glass.

"What happened to your rule? One drink for dinner and one before bed?"

She continued to ignore him and he swallowed his pointless anger. Nothing he said was getting through to her. Perhaps because, in her mind, he was already gone.

"I guess I might as well see myself out." He swiveled and made for the door. She didn't call him back. At the threshold he almost tripped—the damn cat was at his feet again. Swearing, he nudged the feline aside, exited and slammed the door.

The first thing he saw—the mailbox—he jammed his fist into. The thick pewter didn't budge, but his hand exploded in pulses of pain. Then he strode down the walk so quickly he almost bumped into an elderly man walking a furry little white dog.

"Hey, watch where you're going!"

"Sorry..." Dylan stepped over the leash, then searched the darkened street blankly, forgetting for a moment that the shiny gray truck at the curb was his.

The old man and his dog resumed walking, and Dylan glanced back at the house. All the lights were out now. Was his mother drinking in the dark? Or had she switched off the lights so she could see out the window? Not likely. You didn't tell your son you never wanted to see him again, then bother to watch him walk out of your life.

He escaped into the truck, and only once he was seated behind the steering wheel did he feel able to draw in a lungful of air. Why would his mother want to get rid of him so badly? He had to believe she hadn't been speaking for herself, merely repeating the words Max had told her to say.

He searched his memories from a happier past—Christmas mornings, family horseback rides, picnics along the creek. Life had been good when his father was alive. But after marrying Max, his mother had turned her back on all that.

Finally, frustrated, angry, hurt and confused, he headed the truck back to Cathleen's B and B.

"I CAN'T BELIEVE she really wants you to leave," Cathleen said, trying to comfort Dylan the next morning after breakfast. "That's just Max's influence." The front porch had trapped the heat from the morning sun and she felt lethargic as she relaxed against the stair railing. Kip lay in a puddle of sunshine on the wooden floor. Dylan stood, leaning over the porch railing to look across to the Thunder Bar M.

She'd resolved to go easy on Dylan today. He'd appeared so beaten when he came home from his mother's last night, heading straight to his room with barely a word. Only this morning had he been ready to tell her the story.

"No doubt he did." Dylan was on his third, maybe fourth, cup of coffee. The caffeine, from what she could tell, wasn't improving the situation. He seemed jumpy and nervous, tapping the toe of one boot relentlessly against the porch floor.

"Max may have orchestrated the script," Dylan continued, "but she didn't have to deliver it."

"Maybe she felt she had no choice."

"Yeah. I know what you're saying. Believe me, I'm willing to give her the benefit of the doubt. I guess I should be thankful she decided to change her will."

He brought his mug up for another long, apparently satisfying swallow. "Hard not to be bitter, though. I mean, I would do anything to help her, but she insists on staying loyal to that scumbag."

"It *is* hard to understand." But she'd heard enough of Kelly's stories to know that many women found it all but impossible to leave an abusive situation.

Kip raised his head from the porch floor. The next minute Cathleen heard a vehicle approaching. A potential guest? But no, it was Kelly's white police car.

Her sister emerged dressed in uniform, hair pinned up and hidden under her RCMP hat. She looked about as tired and grumpy as Dylan was acting. Something was obviously wrong.

Dylan was just a few steps behind as Cathleen walked briskly to greet her. "Kelly, what happened?" She slipped an arm around her sister's waist and felt a little of Kelly's weight sag against her.

Cathleen checked out her sister's dull coloring, the strands of hair loosened from her regulation plain bun. "Were you working all night? Come on in. I'll make you some breakfast."

"Not yet." Kelly straightened, then settled her gaze on Dylan. "It's bad news, I'm afraid."

Not again! A sudden wind swirled a mass of dry yellow leaves into the air. Dylan stood impervious at the apex of the small whirlwind. In five seconds the air was calm again. Cathleen plucked stray leaves from her sister's uniform. She wanted to beg Kelly to keep quiet, but Dylan had already guessed.

"It's about my mother."

Kelly nodded. "I wanted to get here before the official call." She reached for Cathleen's hand. In turn, Cathleen reached out to Dylan.

"Rose is dead," Kelly said. "It happened last night."

CHAPTER EIGHT

DYLAN COULDN'T BREATHE. It was like being thrown by a bull, only scarier. Because this time there would be no picking himself up and dusting off the dirt.

"That can't be right," he told Kelly. "I was with her last night. And she was fine." Okay, not fine. But *alive*. She'd certainly been that.

"No mistake, Dylan. I am sorry."

As Kelly repeated her apology, there was something in her tone that didn't sound right. Not insincerity, no. But something damn close.

"What happened?" His mother had admitted she'd been seeing specialists in Calgary. Had her heart been weak? Maybe she'd had a stroke. He felt Cathleen's arm go around his shoulders and couldn't stop from tensing. Right now all that mattered were the next words to come out of Kelly's mouth.

"She was shot, Dylan. Death would have been instantaneous."

The blunt words hit him with the impact of a

bullet. He stared until the shock wore off and the meaning sank in.

So it was *murder*. His mother had been murdered.

"Unofficially, the coroner estimates time of death between eight and ten o'clock last night. A next-door neighbor out walking his dog claims he saw you leaving the house at about twenty past eight. He heard some shouting, and says that you left the house in a terrible state."

Dylan saw it then, and suddenly Kelly's weird behavior made perfect sense. She thought *he'd* done it. Killed his own mother.

Well, why not? Just like everyone else in town, she'd never quite believed he wasn't responsible for what happened to Jilly.

Cathleen held both hands to her throat. "Dylan would never hurt his mother. Kelly, this is crazy."

"I couldn't agree with you more. But we have to face facts. You say Dylan couldn't hurt his mother, but what about that night before he left town two years ago? *Someone* gave Rose that awful shiner."

"Kelly! That's not fair. There's no evidence Dylan was responsible that time, either."

The sisters' arguing seemed to come from a great distance. Dylan's senses felt frozen, even as thoughts ricocheted with frightening speed through his mind. The pieces fell into place, so cleanly, so easily, that there could be no doubt what was really going on here.

It all came back to Max, everything. He'd beaten his wife two years ago, and made sure everyone in town drew the false conclusion that Dylan had struck his own mother.

Then, when his fool of a stepson came back to town, he put the rest of his plan into action. Dylan's visit to his mother's had been a setup. Max had asked his wife to call, and had told her exactly what to say. Including the bit about the will? Or had that been his mother's idea of a consolation prize for washing her hands of her son?

Dylan cursed, and swung his fist uselessly in the air. Oh, but he'd been a fool! Why hadn't he been more suspicious of that invitation for a drink? And why hadn't he insisted on taking his mother someplace safe when he'd had the chance?

He'd blown his one and last opportunity to help her. Now it was too late. He paced through the short tufts of wild grass that bordered the lane, hating himself for playing into Max's hand and for not realizing sooner the danger his mother was in.

An unexpected sound had him swinging his head. It was Cathleen, crying into her hands. He took a step forward, wanting to touch her tenderly, to tell her it was okay. The glint in Kelly's eyes stopped him. She put her arm around her sister's shoulders and murmured something he couldn't hear.

Never was it more obvious that Kelly saw him as a dangerous man. And if Kelly thought he was guilty, so would everyone else in Canmore. Maybe even Cathleen this time. She'd believed him about Jilly. But asking her to trust him a second time? That would be too much.

He stopped and let his arm drop to his side. Cathleen gave an anguished cry and turned her face into Kelly's shoulder.

Of course she blamed him. God, he was such a fool. He'd thought coming back and facing down his troubles was the right road to take. But he'd been wrong. Cathleen had been just fine without him. And his mother might still be alive if he hadn't shown up.

When he'd left that hospital in Reno, he should've headed to Texas or maybe Montana and found himself a job on someone else's ranch. He could've given up on his dreams. He didn't have to get married or have those two kids he and Cathleen had always planned on....

She wasn't crying anymore. She'd squared her shoulders. He waited for her to speak, but Kelly was the one to break the untenable silence. She made eye contact with him, her gaze forthright. "They'll be sending someone later to question you."

Cathleen's face got whiter, but she managed to

raise her chin a notch, all the while avoiding his look.

"Maybe I should save them the trouble and turn myself in." It would be better than sitting out here, waiting for them to get in contact with him like last time. He dug in his jeans for the keys to the truck. A few strides got him to the driver's door. He grabbed the handle, warm in the morning sun. The two sisters stood apart now. Cathleen had moved a little closer to him. Briefly their glances coupled, and for the second time that day, his gut bottomed out on him.

He had to close his eyes. The pleading desperation on her face was too much. He didn't know what she wanted, only that whatever it was, he couldn't give it to her. When he was sure he had his emotions under control, he opened his eyes and focused on getting into the truck, inserting the keys, starting the engine.

"Let me come with you."

Even though she thought he was guilty, she was still prepared to stand by him. With all his heart, he longed to lean over and open the passenger door.

But he couldn't do that to her. It was up to him to deal with this. And then bow out of her life, forever this time, when it was over.

At the shake of his head, Cathleen stopped cold. Once again, her sister offered a comforting hand. He was glad she wouldn't be alone when he left.

"If I were you," Kelly said, "I'd get a lawyer before answering any questions."

"Really?" He tipped his hat back from his face a smidgen. "And should I tell him he can call on you as my character witness?"

DYLAN WAS OUT OF HIS TRUCK the second after he'd parked it behind the low brick building that housed the local RCMP detachment. He barged in the main door, half expecting some wily lawman to jump him and handcuff him.

But the receptionist at the front desk, a pleasant young woman with a friendly smile, just asked how she could be of assistance. She stood behind an open window. A locked door was to the left.

"I'm Dylan McLean."

The pretty smile faded. "Rose Strongman's son?"

"So rumor has it." Although Rose had disowned him last night, hours—minutes?—before her death. He couldn't yet believe that she was truly gone. It would take time, a long time, for the loss to sink in.

Right now, though, anger and hate propelled him. All directed at the man who'd stolen his birthright, ruined his good name and now had murdered his mother. His vendetta against Max Strongman had turned into full-fledged war. Till this day, Dylan hadn't truly understood how a man could be in a murderous rage. Now he prayed he wouldn't see Max Strongman in the next twenty-four hours because he couldn't trust himself face-to-face with the man.

"Just one moment, please. I'll get Staff Sergeant Springer." The receptionist backed away and Dylan waited on the wooden bench that ran the length of the small reception area. Minutes later the locked door opened and the clean-cut sergeant dipped his head in acknowledgment.

"Come in, McLean. I've got some questions."

No kidding. Why did Thad think he'd bothered to come here in the first place? Slowly Dylan eased into a standing position. He glanced at Springer's right hand but didn't offer his. The receptionist eyed him cautiously, as if afraid he might draw out a gun and start killing people at random.

Springer led the way past a closed-in glass room filled with computer equipment, then through a large open work area where two men and one woman were sitting at desks, and finally to his office.

"I take it you've spoken to Kelly?" Springer asked.

Dylan nodded impatiently. "Yeah, she told me."

"Okay, then. Sit down. I just have a few questions. You do realize you have the right…"

Springer's routine had Dylan setting his teeth with frustration. He'd been through it once before, after Jilly Beckett's murder, and no longer had any faith in the system or the sergeant. Springer, as far as he could tell, was both nearsighted and unimaginative.

"How's Cathleen?" Springer asked, his expression smug.

"Fine." It was all he could do to get out that one-word answer. Goddamn, he hated knowing that this was one of the men Cathleen had been seeing before he came back to town.

Fighting down an urge to do something about the sergeant's self-satisfied smirk, he studied the man as impartially as he could. Probably in his late thirties, not bad-looking, with boy-next-door features and a big powerful build. *Nice-looking enough, but not Cathleen's type,* he tried to reassure himself.

"I guess now she's sorry she didn't listen to my advice about you," Springer said.

Dylan could imagine what was going through the officer's mind. *Couldn't nail you last time, but now we've got you!* There would be no innocent until proven guilty in this case, Dylan was certain.

"So when did you last see your mother?"

"Why do you ask? You have a witness who saw me leave her house shortly after eight last night. So you know when I last saw my mother, don't you?"

"Don't be a wiseass, Dylan. You know I have to ask these questions."

Dylan shifted positions in the uncomfortable, straight-backed chair. "She'd invited me for a drink. Presumably because Max wasn't home."

"Ah…"

Springer pulled out a notebook and opened to a page near the front. Dylan remembered seeing him follow the same procedure when he was working on Jilly Beckett's homicide. He wondered if Springer had started a nice clean notebook for his mother's case.

Pain crashed in at that thought, and he straightened his back and pulled in his stomach. He couldn't afford to give in to grief, here in the sergeant's chair.

"You and Max don't get along, do you?"

"To put it mildly."

"And what time did you arrive at your mother's?"

"It was close to eight. I left about half an hour later." And Kelly had said his mother had probably died sometime between eight and ten. The timing was too perfect to be coincidental.

Springer's smile was full of satisfaction. "Doesn't look good, McLean."

He'd known he would be a suspect but hadn't expected the sergeant to be so blatant this quickly. "Very cute, Springer. In your mind, I suppose the case is all wrapped up. But what about motive?"

"Ask anyone in town. You and your mother

were at odds. Have been for the past two years. Everyone saw what you did to Rose's face the night before you ran away to become a *rodeo cowboy.*" His tone made the term seem disparaging. "Word around town is that she'd written you out of her will after the Beckett affair."

Dylan pounded the table with his flat hands. "Exactly! And who did she leave the ranch to? Her husband, not me! What, exactly, do you propose I'd be gaining by killing her in these circumstances?"

Especially since his mother had promised to change her will back into her son's favor the next morning. But there was no sense telling that to the sergeant, when Dylan had no way to prove it was true.

"Perhaps you acted out of irrational anger or revenge."

"Or maybe it was Max Strongman who pulled that trigger."

"Really?" Springer set his pen on his desk and closed his notebook.

"Of course he did. He had the perfect motive. With my mother gone, he inherits the ranch, all three thousand acres."

"Not bad incentive," Springer conceded. "But there's one very big flaw in your theory."

"Yeah?"

"While the coroner's word isn't official yet, he's

estimating time of death between eight and ten o'clock that night. Max Strongman was in a town council meeting last night from 7:00 p.m. until midnight. Rose had been dead at least two hours by the time he arrived home.''

"I KNOW DYLAN'S HERE," Cathleen said, trying not to shout. The damn receptionist's evasive tactics made her long to vault over the dividing countertop and push right past her.

"I told you, ma'am. He's in a meeting with the sergeant. I can't interrupt. You'll have to wait until they're finished."

"And I told you, I need to speak with him right this second!" Damn Dylan and his temper. Couldn't he have taken a minute to think things through before rushing to the police station? Without any strategy, he was probably jeopardizing his case and antagonizing the police on top of it.

"Calm down, ma'am. He'll be finished in a few minutes and then you can…"

Livid, Cathleen didn't hear another word. She eyed the locked door to her left and again considered the possibility of leaping over the counter.

Into a room full of police? Really bright idea, Cathleen.

She was pacing the small waiting area five minutes later when the dividing door finally opened. Out came Dylan, color high, features tight with frustrated anger. He jerked to a stop when he saw her.

''What the hell are you doing here?''

She placed her hands on her hips; the posture made her feel bigger, a person to be reckoned with. ''Why did you storm off that way? I thought we were working together on this.''

''Not anymore.'' Dylan slipped past her, heading for the exit. Behind him Cathleen spotted Thad Springer. He'd seen her, too, and looked as if he wanted to talk. Probably he'd give her more answers than Dylan would. But by the time she heard them, Dylan would be gone.

''Cathleen...''

''Later, Thad.'' She swiveled on the ball of her foot and ran after Dylan.

Outside, the morning sun hit her strong and bright. She raised a hand to her forehead and caught sight of Dylan with one foot already inside his truck.

''Where do you think you're going?'' she called out.

When he didn't pause, she raced for the passenger door. She managed to open it and slide into the seat before he could take off.

He yanked the lever back into Park. ''Get out, Cathleen.''

Well. That was blunt enough. She sucked in her

pride. "Not so fast, *darlin'*. Tell me what happened in there. Did you find out anything?"

"This is my problem, not yours. Our 'partnership,' as you called it, officially ended with my mother's death."

"I don't see why. I said I'd help you uncover the truth. I still intend to do that."

Dylan shook his head, narrowed eyes fixed on the brown-red bricks of the RCMP building. "The Beckett homicide was one thing. This is completely different."

She could guess exactly what was eating at him. "What happened to your mother—it's horrible, but not your fault."

"But it is. Don't you see?"

Dylan appeared utterly exhausted. When he finally turned to face her there wasn't a flicker of light in his steel-gray eyes.

"It's almost like Max planned this two years ago when he gave my mother that black eye. He counted on people blaming me. And they did. To my everlasting regret, I played right into his hands when I came home."

"That's so crazy it might just be true. But if Max *is* guilty, we have to stop him. He can't get away with this."

Dylan laughed, a flat, bitter sound. "There's no stopping Max Strongman, darlin'. Haven't you learned that by now?"

She didn't understand his lack of fight. "You can't mean you're not even going to try."

"Cathleen, Max was at a town council meeting when my mother was killed. The RCMP aren't even considering him as a possible suspect."

"Oh no." Now that she thought about it, she knew council meetings were held on the first and third Tuesday of every month. "Then how...?"

"That's the question, isn't it? He must have slipped out of his meeting for however long it took to kill her. Not long. It's a five-minute drive to the house at most." Dylan got out of the truck, and for a moment Cathleen felt a scrap of hope. Maybe they could grab a cup of coffee and brainstorm. Surely between the two of them...

But Dylan had her door open, and his eyes were still cold and shuttered. "Get out of my truck, Cathleen. There's nothing you or anyone else can do now."

"You don't mean that."

"I surely do, darlin'. Go back to your B and B and forget I ever darkened your door."

Stunned, Cathleen slid to the pavement. "Where will you stay?"

"I'm not sure yet. I'm not supposed to leave town. See that constable in his car over there?"

Cathleen nodded. The vehicle was idling. The uniformed driver appeared ready to take off any second.

"He's going to follow me to your place. They want the clothes I was wearing last night. I guess they'll be checking for gunpowder residue. And bloodstains."

And would they find them? Cathleen could see that he was waiting for her to ask the question. Instead, she slammed the door to his truck and kicked the front tire.

"We could have fought this together, you know. If you weren't such an *idiot!*"

But Dylan wasn't listening. He'd gone round to the driver's side again, blocking her out, just like the last time. Faced with a crisis, Dylan McLean stood alone.

"Goodbye, Cathleen."

Anger flowed like a flash flood through her body. "You're a bloody fool, Dylan McLean!" She stomped her boot on the hard concrete sidewalk, then pivoted away from him. Took a few steps, then whirled back. He was in his truck, but the window was open.

"You and your pride...well, I've had enough. I am *so* totally through with you!" She marched off to her own vehicle, pain slashing her heart with every step. Why was this hurting so much? She didn't love Dylan. Those days were over....

Yet, somehow, something must've been rekindled. Or maybe her feelings had never been as extinguished as she'd tried to convince herself.

CHAPTER NINE

THE PHONE RANG THE NEXT morning as Cathleen was getting out of the shower. Quickly wrapping a towel around her body, she raced to the bedside table, her wet feet tracking on the pine flooring.

Don't expect Dylan, she warned herself, and she was right. It was Kelly, calling to see if Cathleen had heard from him.

"No. And I'm not going to. He's moved out. I don't know where he's staying."

"Well, if you see him, phone me. And be careful."

"Be careful of what?" She was really getting tired of this. "Kelly, you know Dylan isn't dangerous."

"Do I? Maybe it's time you did a reality check. When it was only Jilly's death, I was prepared to admit there was a possibility we were wrong. But Dylan is making a habit of hanging out at murder scenes. Besides, who else had both the motive and the opportunity to shoot Rose Strongman?"

"Her husband."

Kelly sighed. "He was at a town council meeting, for heaven's sake!"

"Maybe he slipped out. All it would've taken was fifteen minutes—"

Kelly didn't give her a chance to discuss this theory. She interrupted, her tone gentle yet firm. "Look, it's time you faced the facts, Cath, and let go of all this. Dylan McLean has brought you nothing but grief. I never told you at the time, but when he walked out on your wedding day, a part of me was relieved. I thought then—and I still do—that it was the most honorable thing he could've done."

"Honorable?" She wondered if Kelly would have come to the same conclusion had the facts been reversed. If Cathleen had been the one accused of a crime she hadn't committed, wouldn't Kelly have expected Dylan to stand by her in that case? But there was no sense arguing. The two of them were never going to agree if Kelly thought backing out on a promise of marriage was honorable.

After she'd said goodbye and hung up, though, she stared at the phone for many minutes.

Was she being a fool? Shouldn't she at least consider the possibility that Dylan was guilty? He'd come home from his visit with his mother Tuesday night absolutely exhausted and shattered, refusing to talk to her until the following morning. Perhaps he'd needed the night to collect himself before facing her....

No. It hadn't been that way. Snapping out of her trance, she dressed quickly in her riding clothes, then went out to the stall to saddle Cascade. Besides fixing the sticky door, Dylan had cleaned several days' worth of muck from the floor and replaced the rotting boards that separated the two stalls from each other.

What had he said again? *Indispensable.*

She slumped against the side of Cascade's stall and pressed the back of her hand hard against her eyes. *Do not cry, you wimp.* Filling her lungs with the scent of hay and trapped animal heat, she straightened her shoulders.

"Hey, baby. Want to go for a ride?" Cathleen slapped a hand on Cascade's flank. The quarter horse was a beauty, one of those rare paints with brown markings on a cream background. Cathleen offered a handful of oats she'd scooped from the bin by the door and Cascade crunched them greedily, bumping Cathleen's hand with the end of her nose when they were gone.

"No more right now. I've got plans for you, baby." Cathleen slipped the bit easily into the mare's mouth. Cascade had an amiable nature, but boy, did she love to run. And autumn mornings in the Rockies were meant for running, especially here in Thunder Valley.

Once mounted, Cathleen directed the mare out of the pasture, then paused in anticipation. The peaks of the Three Sisters were newly frosted with snow, the white a perfect contrast to the depthless blue of a cloud-free sky. Looking up, she felt she could see heaven and beyond. Lowering her gaze, she became grounded by the greens and golds of the land, which danced in perfect rhythm with the currents of air streaming from the mountain range to the west.

With Cascade loping, she set out for Thunder Bar M land, awed, as always, by the beauty around her. Out here it was easy to share Dylan's outrage at what Max had done. Not far away was one of the pump jacks erected after successful drilling had established a dozen profitable oil wells on the property.

The mechanical device was in constant motion, arcing forward and backward as it moved the oil inch by inch up the tubing, which probably stretched a kilometer or more into the ground.

Now that the seismic and drilling were completed, the pump jacks were innocuous enough, Cathleen supposed, but that was only if nothing went wrong. Occasionally there were problems that could have major impacts on the soil and the air, and it was primarily for these reasons that Dylan had opposed the expropriation of oil from land he considered a national, as well as a family, heritage.

That Dylan would put his love for the land above

potential for money, lots of money, was just so like him....

Pain burst through the strongholds she'd been trying to build against it. It hit everywhere at once—her heart, her ribs, her stomach. Everything hurt; she almost couldn't stand it. She was so worried about him and so sick of the stubborn independence that Kelly mistakenly considered honor.

Dylan! His name was an explosion of sound that only she could hear. Letting Cascade have her head, she crouched low as they went faster and faster. Wind whipped back her hair and stung her cheeks, and as the blood and adrenaline pounded through her veins to match the rhythm of Cascade's hoofs on the hard ground, she finally felt alive.

Go, baby, go. She urged Cascade on with the merest adjustment of the reins in her hands. The result was magic and Cathleen almost laughed.

But for once the joy of riding Cascade was not enough. Not when there was one question she knew she had to face.

Could Dylan have killed Rose? As Kelly had pointed out, he'd had the opportunity. And he'd most definitely been provoked. As far as she knew, he hadn't been carrying a gun, had never even owned one, but if he had, it wouldn't have been difficult to conceal it from her.

Or to toss it after the crime. Here, in the wilderness, there was no shortage of hiding places: the river, the forest, even a mountain crevasse.

Most damning of all was the way he'd run off yesterday. Not the action of an innocent man. In his favor was the fact that Rose had said she was going to change her will, but he could've lied about that, too....

In her mind, Cathleen accumulated the evidence against him, but no matter how hard she tried, she couldn't change the judgment her heart had already made.

Had Dylan murdered his mother? The answer, most definitely, was no.

CATHLEEN WOULD HAVE preferred not going into Canmore. She didn't want to face any of the people who thought Dylan was guilty and who figured she was a fool for giving him a place to stay even though he'd dumped her so cruelly. But when she returned from her ride, Poppy informed her that they were out of eggs and milk.

"I hope it isn't a bother, but since we need groceries, anyway, could you pick up some pecans for me, as well?" Poppy's hands were immersed in a batch of pastry dough. Red hair tied back with a bright purple ribbon, feet cocooned in gaily embroidered moccasins, she made quite the picture. Cathleen had to smile.

"No problem." She choked down the last bite

of the muffin she'd grabbed on the way in and wondered whether or not to change out of her riding clothes for her trip to town.

As it turned out, she was glad she decided not to bother. At the IGA, several people pretended not to see her in the aisles. Waiting in the checkout line, she eventually began to feel her smile was pasted on her face.

Then at Grazing Grounds, while ordering a large dark-roasted blend to go, she spotted Beth Gibson. The well-groomed woman, whose attractively styled hair contained generous streaks of gray, had been a friend of Cathleen's mother. Cathleen smiled, but the older woman just looked past her.

Cathleen was certain she'd seen her. So why the cold shoulder?

I'll give you three guesses....

Cathleen might have let it go, except that in addition to her full-time job as a real estate agent, Beth was an alderwoman on the town council. After snapping a plastic lid on her paper cup, Cathleen approached the table where Beth was sitting with several local businesspeople. She knew these folks, too, though not as well.

The alderwoman frowned as she drew near but finally, reluctantly, inclined her chin in Cathleen's direction. "Yes?"

"Beth, I need to ask you something."

Dark arched brows moved a fraction closer together. "Go ahead."

Cathleen glanced at the others round the table. "Privately?"

Beth appeared annoyed by the additional request but obliged by leaving her chair and joining Cathleen at a table on the other side of the room.

"I hope this isn't going to be about Rose Strongman, Cathleen."

"Why not?"

"I'd hardly feel comfortable discussing the case with you."

"Oh?"

"You must understand how many of us feel. I admired Rose very much. She, your mother and I were once on the board of the horticultural society together."

"So the changes in her these past few years must have worried you a lot?"

"Well, of course. Rose's deteriorating health was a concern to everyone."

"But did you ever wonder what *caused* her poor health?" Hadn't anyone in this town been observant enough to see what Max Strongman was doing to his wife?

"The cause was obvious, I think," Beth responded. "I've been very lucky with my sons, but many parents have to deal with disappointment over the way their children turn out. Fortunately, few have to live with having raised a criminal. Poor Rose. How she must have agonized over that.''

"Dylan was never charged with Jilly Beckett's murder.''

"No. But we all know what really happened, don't we?'' Beth's mercurial eyes contained not a hint of doubt. "We all felt badly for you, too, Cathleen. Until he came back and you let him stay with you.''

"Beth, Dylan is innocent!''

"Don't be a fool. That man conned you once before. Don't let him do it again.''

As calmly as she could manage, Cathleen removed the plastic lid from her coffee and took a sip. With the cup safely back on the table, she raised another question. "Ever considered the possibility that *you* might be wrong? That someone else could've killed Rose? Someone with more to gain—say, several thousand acres of prime real estate?''

Beth's mouth hardened, emphasizing the lines around her lips. "You'd better be careful who you're accusing, Cathleen. Max Strongman was in a council meeting when Rose was shot.''

"Yes. But did he leave the meeting at any time? You must have taken a break.''

"Of course.''

Cathleen's hopes soared—

''Max and I spent the time together, drinking coffee.''

—and crashed.

Suddenly Beth's features softened and she reached out to stroke Cathleen's hand. ''If your mother were still alive, I'm sure she'd agree with me. Forget about that man, Cathleen. He's bad news. You deserve better.''

LATE THAT NIGHT CATHLEEN pulled the cedar-lined box out from under her bed. For the first time in two years she opened the lid and stared at the contents.

Her thoughts drifted back to the afternoon she'd gone shopping with her sisters in Calgary for a wedding dress. The second she'd emerged from the dressing room, they'd both nodded. ''That's the one.''

She'd known, too, the instant she saw her reflection in the three-way mirror. Just as she'd known Dylan was special since the days when she first began to notice boys. There'd always been an implicit promise between them. Even while she was dating other guys and learning about life. She'd always known Dylan was there, in the background, and that one day it would be serious and it would be forever.

The week after she and Dylan had announced their engagement, Kelly and Maureen had thrown a celebration party. She could remember the three of them catching a moment for a private chat.

"I'm so glad for you, Cath," Kelly had said. "I wish I could find a man who looked at me the way Dylan looks at you. Lucky you. He's got the sexiest smile I've ever seen. And those eyes..."

"Forget that," Maureen had interjected. "The important thing here is that the man is rich!"

Cathleen had howled with laughter at the time. Now she felt the irony. The events of one evening—the evening Jilly had been shot—had changed the opinion of not only her sisters but also the entire town. Dylan had played the part of cowboy gone bad for two years. Now his mother's murder ensured the role was his forever. Unless they could prove someone else was responsible.

Oh, damn him, why had he taken off the way he had? Cathleen kicked the box back under the bed, not bothering to even fold back the tissue paper for a really close look. She *should've* sold this crap the first time he left.

It was late, but she knew she wouldn't sleep. She went to open the window. Just a few centimeters admitted a fresh night breeze that carried the scent of pine and the unceasing babble of water rushing over rocks. Breathing deeply, she thought of all she had to be grateful for: her sisters, her friends, this wonderful home.

She simply wasn't the type of woman who pined

away for a man she knew she couldn't have—talk about *sappy*. And yet, these past few years she'd lived with a low-grade stomachache and a subconscious hope that one day he'd come back. The truth couldn't be denied.

She wasn't over him and she never would be. She loved Dylan McLean.

"Oh, Kip, I'm such a fool, aren't I?" She went to the foot of her bed, where the lab was resting on a corduroy cushion she'd bought from a pet shop in Calgary back when he was a puppy. She was surprised to find him alert, tail wagging, eyes on the open window.

"Jeez. Not again." She'd been about to change out of her clothes. Instead, she paced back to the window and listened. Sure enough, there was the telltale crunch of gravel. Someone was driving slowly down the lane.

Quickly she switched off the lamp by the side of her bed and sat on the cushioned window seat. Approaching headlights stopped, then flickered out, about fifty meters from the house. She concentrated on the moonlit landscape and, after several minutes, saw a masculine figure emerge from the vehicle.

She had little doubt it was Dylan. He advanced toward the house, and as he drew nearer, her heart rate accelerated.

What did he want? What would he say to her? After about fifteen minutes, she realized she was never going to know the answers to those questions. Dylan wasn't planning on coming up to the house. He'd stopped about twenty meters from the side porch, and from the angle of his head, she guessed he was looking straight into her window.

Cathleen fought the urge to duck. The room was dark; no way could he see in. So it was safe for her to sit and watch him, and she did for almost half an hour.

What was he thinking? Why was he standing there?

She was struck by how alone he was. Was he scared? In his shoes, she would have been, although she probably wouldn't admit it. Just as he wouldn't, either.

They were alike in so many ways—stubborn and proud. Maybe it was a good thing fate had separated them. No, she wouldn't blame fate. It was Max Strongman and his greed. Profits from the oil wells on the Thunder Bar M weren't enough. He'd wanted the land, as well, and his freedom, to boot. So he'd killed his wife. Or arranged for someone else to kill her.

And now the man she loved was being blamed for the crime. God, she couldn't bear it. He'd already suffered so much. She hated to think that he now blamed himself for Rose's death. For certain she knew he wouldn't take credit for any of the things he'd done to try to help his mother.

Dylan had been standing in the dark for so long she was startled when he turned abruptly and headed back to his truck. She panicked.

If he left now, who knew when she'd see him again? Without stopping to reason things out, Cathleen ran out her door and down the stairs, then through the hall to the kitchen. Her boots echoed loudly on the wooden porch floor, catching Dylan's attention.

He glanced behind him, and she waved her arms. "Hang on a minute, you idiot! I've got to talk to you!"

CHAPTER TEN

"DYLAN! WAIT!" Once she hit the ground, Cathleen began to run flat out. He was already at his truck. But he'd seen her. Surely he wouldn't drive away.

For a second, it seemed he would. He disappeared into the front seat and she felt like screaming. Then, inexplicably, he stepped out again.

She stopped.

"Cathleen, go back to the house. I shouldn't have come here."

She ignored that. "Where have you been? The police have been looking for you."

Dylan removed his hat, set it on the cab roof and finger-combed his thick hair. On long, lean legs he stepped into a pool of moonlight on a patch of the road. His weariness was palpable as he paused, his voice uncharacteristically flat when he spoke.

"Yeah? Well, they found me. I'm camping at Dead Man's Flats."

The nearby campground, right off the Trans-Canada, was such a logical place for him to take refuge that she couldn't believe she hadn't thought of it herself.

"I didn't know you had a tent."

"Bought one yesterday. Plus a sleeping bag and propane stove. You should see my setup. Real cozy."

Cathleen wasn't deceived by his attempt to be lighthearted. He was shattered. Absolutely shattered. Well, of course. His mother was dead and the police suspected him. She couldn't stand it anymore.

"Oh, Dylan..." She moved toward him with a sense of inevitability. By the time she reached him, his arms were open.

"I shouldn't be here," he muttered again, but he only held her tighter.

Oh, this felt so good. She pressed her face to the muscles of his good shoulder, seeking his heat, his scent, the comfort of his face resting on the top of her head.

"They're going to arrest me this time," he said.

She pressed down her own panic. "They don't have any evidence."

"They'll find it. Concoct it. Do whatever they need to get me behind bars."

She squeezed tighter. "I won't let you go. I love you, Dylan. You will not go through this alone."

I love you. Had he noticed?

"Cathleen?"

He eased his hold a little and she lifted her head so he could see into her eyes. She didn't try to conceal anything from him this time. Her sadness, her ache, her love.

"Cathleen." He swallowed, clenched his jaw, blinked. "Oh, my God, Cathleen."

THE CANDLES IN HER BEDROOM projected flickers of gold onto her white ceiling. Dylan's chest glimmered above her, hard and smooth like polished maple, except for the scars.

Cathleen placed her hand gently on his shoulder, where he'd been injured. "Is it aching?"

"How could it? I'm with you."

Dylan devoured her with his eyes, the way he'd devoured her with his kisses earlier. It was the look, she knew, that Kelly had spoken of with slight envy, an aeon ago when Dylan's reputation had been above reproach.

She arched her pelvis slightly, wanting him deeper, closer. His moan of pleasure tangled in her hair.

"I've loved you forever," he said.

"I know." She lowered her body back onto the bed, plateauing their pleasure and prolonging the moment. Across the room, their images were captured perfectly in the oval of an antique mirror. Glistening limbs, tensed muscles, flowing hair...

She caught his gaze in the reflection and asked quietly. "Ready?"

He nodded and, still facing the mirror, resumed making love to her. In her ears, blood pounded out a steady rhythm that grew faster and louder, to match the surging pleasure.

At the end, they turned back to each other, gasps silenced as their mouths crushed together. For a full minute the echoes of that final crescendo reverberated through Cathleen's limp body.

"Don't be sorry," Dylan murmured, brushing her hair with one hand, over and over. The shadows from the candlelight brought out the angle of his cheekbones, the sharp edge of his jaw.

"I'm not," she reassured him, burying her own doubts in order to protect him. As long as he wasn't looking for promises, she would stay and see him through these days. And accept the fact that this decision would only mean more pain for her in the long run.

ROSE STRONGMAN'S FUNERAL was well attended for several reasons. First, she'd been the wife of a local rancher. Bud McLean's grandfather had staked his claim in Thunder Valley back in 1837, when the town was nothing more than a few buildings and a dirt road. Bud's friends were the loyal, long-standing type, and even though his widow had remarried, they remembered her hospitality during the years she'd been a rancher's wife, and they wanted to honor her.

Second, because she'd been the wife of the mayor, her death drew all the important business and government citizens in the town.

Then there were the people who'd never known Rose, or either of her two husbands, people with no social or political obligation. The curious, the fascinated, drawn by the drama of a small-town murder.

It was for all these reasons that Dylan's mother's funeral made attendance records at the Ralph Connor United Church—and Dylan refused to go.

"If I show up, the service will turn into a circus," he said. "Besides, I don't think I'm ready to lay eyes on Max Strongman yet."

Cathleen knew he meant that he wouldn't be able to see Max without also feeling the urge to throttle the mayor with his bare hands.

"Let her friends and neighbors honor her in their way and I'll stick to mine."

They purchased a Colorado spruce from a nearby tree farm and hauled it in the back of Dylan's truck to the old family graveyard where Bud McLean was buried. A small dirt road led off from the main road. Dylan stopped his truck behind a grove of trembling aspen.

The cold night had brought a morning frost, and now, in the fresh sunshine, the golden aspen leaves were falling like rain, as if the trees had become suddenly impatient with their summer foliage.

"Listen." Cathleen put a hand to Dylan's arm. The swooshing of the falling leaves was gentle yet relentless, like mourners rustling their clothing and funeral programs, before the minister begins to speak.

"Perfect, isn't it?" Dylan pulled a spade from the back of the truck and then took her hand, leading her to his father's plot. The headstone was local sandstone; the inscription simple: *Bud McLean, 1937-1985, Son of the land. Beloved father and husband.*

"What about here?" Dylan had the spade positioned a meter left of his father's burial space.

Cathleen assessed the spot, imagining the tree at maturity. Would it catch enough light to grow? Would there be room? She nodded. "That's fine, Dylan. I'll get the water."

They'd filled two clear water carriers at home from the outside tap. She brought them one at a time, setting them close to Dylan, who was really putting his back into his work. The ground was hard, and the tree they'd selected large enough to require a fairly big hole.

After a few minutes he paused, resting one foot on the spade. The expression in his eyes, shaded by the brim of his Resistol, was reflective. "I always figured my mother would be buried here, beside my father. Even after her marriage to Max, that was what I thought would happen.''

But it wasn't to be. Dylan had phoned the local funeral director when the RCMP told him they were releasing the body to the family. They'd informed him that Max had requested a cremation and that he planned to dispose of the ashes himself. Cathleen knew Dylan would like nothing better than to scatter those ashes here, but the chances that Strongman would cooperate with such a request were not worth considering.

Dylan began digging again. The harsh rasp of metal against packed earth drowned out the sound of the leaves and the early-morning birds. Above the treetops, Cathleen saw the vee-formation of a flock of Canada geese heading south. The natural world was preparing for winter; in a sense, she and Dylan were doing the same.

Their reunion was like a glorious Indian summer. In September, when the sun shone and the sky was blue and the leaves sparkled, it was hard to believe the snow and cold and blasting winds were only weeks away.

Cathleen didn't want to think about winter, her winter, fast approaching. Instead, she strolled among the tombstones, pausing longest at the ones for children. Dylan had had an elder sister, who'd been born with a defective heart and had died at age three. Poor Rose had lived through some sad, heartbreaking troubles. Losing her daughter, then her husband at the prime of her adulthood.

Running the ranch and raising a teenage son must have seemed overwhelming to Rose then. No wonder she'd been drawn to a man like Max, who must have struck her as both strong and self-reliant. Only later could she have realized the extent to which he planned to control and dominate her.

"There, that's done." Dylan laid down his shovel and Cathleen came back to help him dump both containers of water into the fresh hole. Most of it leached quickly into the earth, but a small puddle remained by the time Dylan had fetched the tree, roots still wrapped loosely in burlap.

"Tell me if it's straight."

Cathleen stood back as he lowered the tree into the ground. "A little to the left." She moved in a semicircle, inspecting from all angles. "Okay, that's good."

Together, they piled soil to cover the roots, until the tree was solidly anchored. Cathleen thought of her own mother's funeral, how she and both of her sisters had tossed that final, symbolic handful of earth on top of the pine coffin. At this moment, she felt that same somber, heart-heavy sadness. She reached for Dylan's hand, and he held on tightly.

"Rose Lamont McLean, this tree is in memory of the woman, the wife and the mother you once were." The simple words were all he could manage. Cathleen shuffled closer and put her arm round his shoulders. Together they sat, merely sat, and felt the loss of one special woman from the world.

MAKING LOVE WITH CATHLEEN the second night was just as emotionally and sexually intense as the night before, but in a different way. This time Dylan sensed her vulnerability more than her strength. He responded with tenderness, and later he would have continued to stroke her and tell her he loved her all night if she'd have let him. But around eleven she fell asleep, exhausted from the long day. Dylan wanted nothing more than to lose himself to slumber while holding her in his arms. But he couldn't get his mind to gear down.

He hated to think of all that Cathleen was risking to be with him. If he were a stronger man, he would have turned his back on her the other night, returned to the campground and never given in again to this crazy, all-consuming urge to be near her.

If only the two of them could run away together, leave this town and these people and start fresh someplace new....

But even that dream was elusive, because he knew it wasn't the answer. Cathleen had too much holding her here, especially her sisters. And he had his ranch, the Bar M, his identity. Working the rodeo for two years had taught him nothing if not where he truly belonged in this world.

Worried that his tossing and turning would wake Cathleen, Dylan eased his body up from the mattress, dressed quickly and went out to his truck. It was a dumb idea, but he couldn't stop himself from heading toward Canmore and cruising past Strongman's house. Slowly he circled the cul de sac, then parked several houses away from the stucco abomination.

More than anything, he wanted to walk up to that front door and ring the bell. When Max appeared, he would plow his fist into the mayor's self-satisfied face.

Revenge. How badly he wanted to make that man pay for all he'd done to his mother in the years of their marriage.

But he couldn't afford a hotheaded maneuver like that. If he was going to even the score with his stepfather, it had to be on a legal battlefield. But Max, with his impossibly perfect alibi, would be a tough man to defeat.

And the creep knew it. Dylan could just imagine him playing the role of grieving widower today. How he would've soaked up the attention of his friends and colleagues. Those friends and colleagues were probably long gone now. The house was mostly dark save for one bank of windows on the main floor. Perhaps Max was reading the paper or watching late-night TV. Undoubtedly he was reveling in how well his plans had worked out.

Dylan wanted to let him know that not everyone was deceived by that polished facade of his. He wanted to tell him that his days were numbered. That Rose's son would make sure he paid for his crimes.

Only it didn't seem possible that he could. Max was either damned lucky, bloody smart or both. As far as Dylan could tell, the RCMP weren't even considering Max a suspect. No, all their suspicions were focused on him—the prodigal son, whose return had inspired not even so much as the opening of a can of lima beans.

The front door of the Strongmans' house opened suddenly and two men appeared on the landing, one large, the other slight. Dylan slunk back into his seat, observing in comfortable darkness. The larger man—Max—patted the slightly built guy on the back.

"Good work, boy. I'll be talking to you soon." Max wasn't speaking loudly, but in the still night air, his deep voice carried.

The visitor muttered something in reply, then turned toward the street. He was dressed in scruffy jeans and a T-shirt. His light-brown hair was on the longish side, and unbrushed. As he stepped out to the street, the light from a sconce on one side of the triple garage doors revealed his face.

Danny Mizzoni, the man Max had hired to look

after the Bar M. Odd that he should be one of the latest mourners.

Dylan watched the skinny man walk down the sidewalk, wondering where he was headed. Only two vehicles were parked on the street, a navy Volvo and a Land Rover much like Max's, only a more current model. Both were much too posh for Danny.

And yet, Danny made a beeline to the Rover, keys in hand. He unlocked the front door and got behind the wheel with all the authority of a legal owner. Now, how in the world had Danny managed to afford a pricey set of wheels like that? Dylan hadn't noticed the Land Rover at the ranch when he and Cathleen had stopped by last week.

As Danny drove past him down the street, Dylan dropped low behind the steering wheel, hoping the young man wouldn't notice him in the dark. Since his truck was new, even if Danny glanced at it, he wouldn't associate it with him.

Dylan waited a few minutes before turning on the ignition. About to pull out into the street, he spotted a patch of white on the road ahead. With a twist of his fingers, his headlights blazed. Suddenly two eerie, glowing eyes were staring back at him. He started, then laughed at himself. It was only the damn cat. What had his mother called her? Precious? No, Crystal, that was the name.

Remembering his mother's panic at the possibility the cat might have escaped outside, he figured Crystal wasn't used to the outdoors. The way she was sitting in the middle of the road, like a target, confirmed his hunch.

Dylan opened the door and called out softly. ''Here, kitty, kitty.'' To his surprise, the white cat responded immediately. A second later, she sat perched on the passenger seat beside him, licking a paw, then rubbing her face.

On the drive home Dylan tried to remember if Cathleen liked cats.

CHAPTER ELEVEN

"I'M A *DOG* PERSON, DYLAN. Dog people don't get along with cats," Cathleen said the next morning as she scavenged an old bowl from the cupboard, then wondered what to do about food. Perched on the kitchen floor, Crystal waited very politely for her breakfast, while Kip pouted in the corner by the screen door.

"What were my choices?" he asked her. "I have a feeling Max set her outside on purpose. Maybe he was hoping she'd get run over or lost."

"Do you think?"

"I wouldn't put it past him."

Cathleen sighed. She didn't really mind about the cat, although the new pet might pose problems for potential guests with allergies. Crystal did have a certain elegant aura. She'd add a touch of class to the place.

"Here." She held up a squat can of flaked tuna triumphantly. "I just found breakfast."

Dylan opened the tin, then scooped out a few tablespoons for the feline.

They were passing time, waiting for Rose's accountant, Harvey Tomchuk, to arrive for coffee. Dylan had called him on the off chance that his mother might have discussed with him her plans to alter her will.

"How did you know Harvey Tomchuk was the Strongmans' accountant?" Cathleen asked. Dylan had relayed his last conversation with his mother almost word for word. Rose had said her accountant was someone she trusted. She hadn't, however, provided an actual name.

In worn jeans and a plain white T-shirt, his dark hair only cursorily brushed, Dylan was sexier than any man Cathleen had ever seen. She kissed him full on the mouth, then let him answer.

"That day we went to visit my mother, I took a peek in the mailbox. A thick envelope had Harvey Tomchuk's return address in the corner. So I figured…"

"You *are* sneaky," she said approvingly. "Back to Danny, I *do* find it very suspicious that you saw him leaving Max's house so late. Danny doesn't seem like the kind of guy who bothers to pay his respects to anyone. I wouldn't put it past him to miss his own mother's funeral, let alone go to someone else's. Besides, he hardly knew Rose."

"My bet he was there on business."

"At close to midnight?"

"The kind of business it's safer to conduct at night." Dylan took a plastic container she passed him and scraped the leftover tuna inside. "I'm not sure if a man with Max Strongman's profile knows how to get a handgun. Danny would, though. Hell, maybe Max paid Danny to do the whole thing. That would explain Mizzoni's new Land Rover."

"Paid him? You mean like a mercenary?" The concept was revolting. But no more revolting, she supposed, than doing the murder firsthand.

"Exactly so."

Cathleen shivered, even as she mentally acknowledged that this could be good news for Dylan's case. If they could *prove* Danny was involved...

"Maybe we should have a chat with Mr. Danny Mizzoni."

"Let's do that after Harvey leaves." Dylan checked the time on the microwave display. "He should be here any minute."

Cathleen took the plastic container from Dylan and stored it in the fridge. Crystal tore into the tuna with deep-throated meows of pleasure. Kip watched, it seemed, with some resentment. Feeling sorry for the old guy, Cathleen gave him a treat of his own.

"Will Harvey tell us anything useful?"

"I'm sure he can't talk indiscriminately about his clients. But my mother seemed to trust him. If there's something we should know, hopefully he'll find a way to get it across."

KIP STARTED BARKING about ten minutes later, announcing the arrival of their guest. Dylan stood up from the kitchen table, where he and Cathleen were supervising Poppy as she glazed the fruit buns she'd baked that morning.

He went out the screen door to the veranda, waving for Harvey to come on inside. The retirement-age accountant was a short, spry man, with thick white hair and the kind of blue eyes that always seemed to be sparkling, even when he wasn't smiling, such as now.

"Dylan. I'm glad to see you. Sorry I haven't stopped by earlier." Harvey held out his hand when he was close enough, and Dylan shook it gladly, amazed that there was someone in Canmore who didn't consider him an outcast.

"Let's go inside," he said. "Cathleen wants to say hi, and her guest, Poppy O'Leary, has just pulled some fresh baking out of the oven."

Harvey said a warm welcome to Cathleen, then eyed Poppy with interest as they were introduced. In a matter of a few minutes, the two older people discovered that they'd both been born in the Maritimes.

"I left when I was a young man, lured by the mountains," Harvey confessed. "Although my plan has always been to return to the sea when I retire. How about you? How did you end up almost halfway across the country from your home?"

"Home is all about family. And none of mine was still living in Halifax when I decided to leave. I'm not sure when, if ever, I'll go back," Poppy said.

Dylan noticed Cathleen listening with interest. Poppy rarely talked about herself. Cathleen had told him once that she thought something very sad had happened in Poppy's past because she avoided the topic so carefully.

After Poppy had served her buns, along with mugs of freshly brewed coffee, she exited discreetly. Harvey immediately turned the subject to more personal matters.

"I'm so sorry about your mother, son. In her final years, I was one of her few friends. In fact, I spoke to her the day she died."

Dylan felt as if his last swallow of food had balled up in his throat. He needed a moment to find his voice. "I'm glad to hear she had a friend, Harvey."

"I wish I'd been a better one." Harvey tapped a spoon against the edge of his mug. "I feel so terrible about what happened to her. That morning when she spoke to me on the phone, I could tell she was distressed."

"May I ask what she wanted to talk about?"

"She wanted me to arrange a visit with her lawyer. She insisted no one else know. My guess is that it was Max she was worried about."

So his mom *had* been serious about changing her will. "How well do you know Max?"

"I've been his accountant since he married your mother. But I've never felt right about the financial arrangements between the two of them. Not that I'm in a position to make public comments."

Dylan glanced at Cathleen. "We understand."

"I helped your mother a lot during those first years after your father died. She didn't have much confidence, but she was a smart woman. The decisions she started making after she married Max, though—" Harvey shook his head "—they weren't smart. The way they had their affairs set up, all her profits from her investments and oil properties accrued to her husband."

"Did you try talking to Mom?"

"I did. I told her it wasn't right, that she had to protect her own interests. And yours. Nothing I said made any difference...."

"Well, you're not the only one she wouldn't listen to."

"You tried, as well?"

"Not about the money. Frankly, I couldn't care less about that. Since I've been back I've had the distinct impression that Max wasn't just controlling the finances in that household. I think he was physically abusive, also. I tried to talk to Mom about it, but she wouldn't hear a word spoken against him."

"I was beginning to wonder about that possibility,'' Harvey admitted. ''Just about every time I went to the house to see her she had bruises somewhere or other. I was curious about how she got them, when she hardly ever left the house.''

''Do you think she was afraid to face people because...because she was ashamed of me?''

''Oh no.'' Harvey's face softened compassionately. ''In my opinion, Max encouraged her to stay home. By effectively cutting her off from the rest of the world, he increased his influence over her proportionately.''

''What an evil man,'' Cathleen said. ''Why didn't I realize what was happening sooner? It all seems so obvious now. And yet there are others who still don't believe it.''

''Such as the police?'' Harvey guessed.

''Exactly.'' Dylan decided to take a chance and trust Harvey with his theory. ''I've been wondering if Max himself was behind my mother's death. Of course, the RCMP think I'm crazy. Max was in a council meeting that night, which doesn't help.''

''I don't think you're crazy,'' Harvey said. ''But the council meeting does present a pretty good alibi.''

''Max could've slipped out for fifteen or twenty minutes,'' Cathleen said. ''Or maybe he paid someone...''

''Like Danny Mizzoni,'' Dylan added.

''Danny Mizzoni.'' Harvey whistled softly as he

considered the possibility. "An unsavory character, to be sure. He hasn't got a record of violence, though."

"True," Cathleen said. "But he'd have the connections to get a gun for Max, wouldn't he?"

"Now, that I definitely wouldn't put past him," Harvey said. "To be indiscreet—but hopefully for a good cause—Max made a curious decision to liquidate some of his investments lately, which I puzzled over. The timing was wrong, you see. He'd have made a much bigger profit if he'd continued to hold them."

"Oh?" Dylan could tell Cathleen was as intrigued as he was. "Can you tell us how much money was involved?"

"Close to a hundred thousand dollars."

Dylan whistled. "More than enough to buy a new Land Rover."

"What?" Harvey asked.

"Last night I noticed Danny was driving a new Land Rover. I wondered how he could afford it."

"That *is* suspicious. It wouldn't hurt to ask the RCMP to look into this." He started rapping his mug with his spoon again. "But you can't tell them about the liquidated investments. I'll deny having said anything."

"Fair enough. Believe me, Harvey, I don't want to get you in trouble." Dylan rose from the table and wandered to the window. Outside, the hills of the Thunder Bar M were frustratingly close. He wanted to be encouraged by what Harvey was telling him, but past experience had made him cautious. He rinsed his mug, then placed it in the dishwasher. Turning back to Harvey and Cathleen, he voiced his concerns.

"I don't know if it would matter, anyway. The RCMP don't seem very interested in following leads in my mother's murder. Unless they involve *me*."

AFTER HARVEY LEFT, Cathleen and Dylan drove out to the Bar M. Their plans to talk to Danny were thwarted when Sharon explained that her husband had gone to Calgary for the day on business.

"What sort of business?" Dylan asked bluntly. Sharon claimed not to know, but her mannerisms indicated nervousness. Was she lying about Danny or worried about something else? Despite his curiosity, Dylan knew he'd have to wait until the next day for the answers.

That night, he and Cathleen had the B and B to themselves. Harvey had phoned about an hour after he'd left them to ask Poppy out for dinner. He'd picked her up at seven and whisked her off to the Post Hotel in Lake Louise—definitely one of the more impressive restaurants in the area. Dylan had to admit, the accountant had style.

"What do you want to do for dinner?" Cathleen

stood in front of the open fridge, one hand perched on her hip. "We've got steaks thawed."

"Maybe later." He wrapped his arms around her, then tilted her head back. "We've got the house to ourselves, darlin'. Let's do a little exploring."

They made love in the study—something Dylan had fantasized about since he'd first seen her prop her booted feet up on the filing cabinet. After, the idea of a little food appealed to both of them.

"Let's eat in the dining room. Make it all fancy," Cathleen suggested. She set out good china and crystal while Dylan took care of the barbecue and made a salad. Once the steaks were on the grill, she went upstairs to change.

Dylan kept busy while he was waiting, lighting a blaze in the fireplace.

When she finally came down the stairs, all he could do was stare. She had on a wispy cranberry-colored, strapless number. The dress itself was incredibly sexy, but the finishing touch was that she'd chosen to wear it without shoes or stockings. Or anything else, he was willing to bet.

"Something's burning," she said, her eyes meeting his.

"It isn't dinner."

She avoided his hand as he reached for her, instead slipping over to the table with a package of matches. It was almost ten now, dark outside and cool. The heat from the fire warmed the room nicely.

Dylan stood at the far end of the table, waiting as she lit the candles. One by one she set the tapers alight. Partway through, she glanced at him, and he felt a sudden, torturous stab of guilt.

"What's wrong?"

"You're so beautiful. You could have any man you want." He gripped the back of a chair, turning his knuckles white.

"I want you." She touched a match to the final wick. Once the flame was established, she shook the match, then tossed it into the fireplace.

He flicked off the electric lights, and the mood in the room changed instantly, became somber, almost threatening. The flames in the fireplace and from the candles on the table pulsed with their own life energy. The windowpanes rattled against a growing wind.

"Don't you ever wonder if you might be wrong about me?" he asked. "Maybe the people of Canmore are right to have their suspicions."

Cathleen froze. With her hair flowing to her shoulders, one hand raised to the ivory smoothness of her throat, she looked like the heroine in a movie about vampires.

He'd frightened her. Even knowing it, he couldn't stop himself.

"Ever wake up in the middle of the night with

me by your side and find yourself wondering if I could've done it?''

"No," she whispered.

"I was there that night. Alone in that house with my mother. I could've hidden a gun in my truck, snuck it inside under my jeans jacket, shot my mother. Maybe I killed Jilly Beckett, too. It's *possible,* Cathleen.''

"No." She said it louder this time. "Don't try to frighten me, Dylan. It won't work.''

But for a second it had. There was a new uncertainty in her eyes, which hurt him all the more for knowing he'd put it there.

"Don't talk that way," Cathleen continued. "You have to have faith. We're going to beat this. We really are.''

Dylan paused, lowering his head. Was she trying to convince him or herself? He was the last person on earth to judge.

"I'd better get the steaks," he said. "I know you like them rare.''

CATHLEEN COULDN'T TASTE the meat, although it had been cooked perfectly. She couldn't taste the wine or the salad, either. Her senses were too caught up by the currents between her and Dylan. Somehow fear had turned into sexual tension. Since the moment she'd walked down the stairs, she'd known Dylan was dying to get her out of her dress. She wanted the same thing.

They ended up leaving their plates half full. Dylan blew out the candles, then undressed her in the light from the fireplace. Feeling his hands brush over her skin sent her desire to a knee-weakening level. She wanted to collapse onto the floor right there. Make love in the warm light of the fire. But he insisted they prolong their pleasure by taking a dip in the hot tub first.

They managed to stay in the heated water for only a few minutes before Dylan picked her up and carried her onto the deck.

The chilled night air was like a balm against her burning skin. She didn't know whether her desire or the hot tub had elevated her temperature. But she knew what she needed. And that was Dylan. Cathleen tipped her head back and let her hair fall away from her face.

He held her securely against his hard, hot body. Dropping her head to his shoulder, she squeezed her arms tightly. If only there was a way to freeze moments in time so that later you could go back to them. This was one of those moments that she wanted to capture forever.

"Where are you taking me?" she asked as Dylan started walking.

"Not far. Cathleen, I need to hold you and make love with you. Now."

His sudden urgency reminded her of that strange moment in the dining room when he'd turned out the lights. Dylan had scared her with his talk about how he *might* have killed his mother. It was as if he *wanted* her to doubt him.

They made it as far as the teak lounge chair, where they'd dropped their robes earlier. Dylan laid her out gently on the soft terry cloth, then propped himself above her. With his legs between hers, his upper body supported by his arms, he gazed down at her.

"This is all I have to offer you," he said, before lowering his mouth to kiss her.

Cathleen kept her eyes open. The moment their lips met, her fear disappeared completely. She pulled his body closer, eager for the moment when he would come alive inside her.

Let me love you. Let me believe in you. His body was hot and damp and fully aroused. To her he was perfect, even the deep scar in his shoulder, where his flesh had been trampled by the bull.

They kissed as if life itself depended on it. Their bodies strained, then met. She touched his face. *I love you.* She knew he loved her, too. It was enough for the moment, but not enough for forever. If that made her a fool, at least she was a willing one.

CHAPTER TWELVE

AFTER HER RIDE ON CASCADE the next morning, Cathleen didn't bother to change out of her jeans and riding boots but just picked up her purse and keys from the hooks by the side door. Poppy was on the phone in the kitchen. Judging by the color in her cheeks and the smile dancing on her lips, Harvey Tomchuk was on the other end of the line.

Cathleen waved, then slipped back outside. Last night's high winds had brought a change of weather to the mountains. Today's hot temperatures were reminiscent of summer and carried the promise of thundershowers later in the day.

Dylan was in the driveway, washing his new truck. His bare back gleamed in the midmorning sun and his old faded jeans rode low on his hips. Looking at him, she felt a strange premonition.

Thad Springer had called earlier with more questions, keeping up the pressure on Dylan. She'd left the room to give Dylan privacy, but not before she'd heard a few curt replies that had made it plain Thad was on the offensive.

It was time for her to sound out her sister, and

hopefully pose a few alternatives that might get this investigation moving in a more fruitful direction.

"I'm off to see Kelly." She dangled the Jeep keys in one hand as she reached over the spray of the hose to kiss him on the mouth.

"Mmm." Dylan released her after a few seconds. "Have fun."

She rolled her eyes, knowing she would have to endure another sisterly lecture. "Wait for me before you go see Danny."

"I will."

"Promise?" she insisted.

"Already waited two years for you, didn't I?"

Cathleen pulled open the door to the Jeep. "You weren't the one who was waiting. I was."

"Oh? So now you finally admit it?"

Caught, she could only laugh. Dating other men had never put a dent in her feelings for Dylan. To pretend otherwise now was pointless. She slid into the driver's seat, blowing Dylan one more kiss. He jumped in the air to catch it.

Ten minutes to Canmore didn't give her much time to think about how she would broach the conversation with Kelly. In town she parked in front of the Bagel Bites Café. Kelly was already seated at one of the two chairs in front of the gas fireplace when she walked in.

"Hello, Sis. How are you?" Cathleen straddled the chair, taking in her sister's pulled-back hair, her well-pressed uniform. Kelly managed to carry off the severe look with a calm beauty.

"Fine. Here's your coffee." Kelly nudged a ceramic mug toward Cathleen.

"I see you're on duty…?"

"More of the usual."

"Aren't you working on the homicide?" Cathleen had imagined the entire detachment would be focusing on the crime.

"Off and on. Right now I'm on coffee break from my usual patrol." Kelly fiddled with the herbal tea bag in her own hot drink.

"Oh. I was hoping you might be able to fill me in on what's been happening."

"I figured that was why you called."

"Other than wanting to see my baby sister, of course." Cathleen patted Kelly's cheek, as if she were still a little girl. Funny how the youngest in the family had turned out so responsible and serious. Cathleen still couldn't believe she had a sister who was a cop.

"I doubt it," Kelly said. "Everyone in town knows what's going on at your place."

Jolted by her sister's tone, Cathleen tensed. "Such as—"

"You're—you're—*sleeping* with him. Aren't you?"

Cathleen just had to roll her eyes. Despite its population of more than ten thousand people, at times Canmore seemed so small-town. "Yes, Dylan and I are lovers, if that's what you're asking."

"I could tell the minute you walked into the café." Kelly looked as stricken as if Cathleen had taken on a life of crime.

"Was it the red *A* sewn onto my shirt?" Kelly didn't even smile. Humor never worked on her when she was in one of these moods.

"Tell me something, Cath. How many guests have checked into your B and B since Dylan moved in?"

Surprised by the question, Cathleen thought back to the night she'd accepted Dylan's check and realized she hadn't touched the receipt book since.

"None," she admitted.

"And what does that tell you?"

She knew the point Kelly was trying to make and refused to give in. "It's slow season...."

"Have you ever gone a full week without so much as one guest booking?"

"No, but—"

"Local business establishments have stopped giving your number out. When potential customers ask about your place, they're encouraged to go elsewhere. You think I'm making this up? I tell you, it's true. I have it from Thad Springer. He doesn't want to see you lose your business. And you *could*, Cathleen, if this goes on much longer."

"I've still got Poppy. And Dylan, of course."

"But what about the future? Who's going to rent their rooms once they move on?"

"I can't worry about that now." Getting through each day was hard enough without planning for the ones to follow. Especially when it came to Dylan. They were loving each other on borrowed time and Cathleen couldn't stand to contemplate the day when it would end.

Kelly clicked her tongue impatiently. "Why won't you take this situation more seriously?"

"And do what? Kick Dylan out?"

"Well, yes. That's what I think you should do."

Cathleen pushed her chair back. She was leaving; she didn't have to put up with this. "Who I sleep with is no one's business but mine."

Liquid splashed out of the mugs on the table as Kelly reached up to grab her arm. "Don't you go running out on me."

"What?" Trapped by her sister's grip, Cathleen stood still. A deep breath gave her the strength to be calm. "Let go."

"Only if you sit down and listen for a minute."

To more lectures? Cathleen groaned. "Kelly, whatever you say isn't going to make any difference."

"Maybe not. But use your head, for just a minute. We're talking murder here. *Murder*. It doesn't get more serious than that. I understand you love him, but couldn't you wait...?"

"I don't need to wait. I already know. And you will, too, once you hear the latest." Cathleen leaned over the table and dropped her voice to a whisper.

"The night of Rose's funeral, Dylan saw Danny Mizzoni leave Max's house very late at night. And guess what? Danny was driving an expensive new Land Rover."

"So?"

"There's more. Yesterday we found out that Max recently liquidated about a hundred thousand dollars' worth of investments."

"I repeat, so?"

"Come on, Kelly. Maybe Max used that money to pay Danny for something...something very risky and highly illegal."

"Oh, Cath! There could be dozens of legitimate reasons for Max to have cashed in his investments. As for Danny's new wheels, isn't it more likely he financed the purchase with more drug money? We've been watching him lately, just waiting for him to slip up. He's become smarter since his last stint in jail, unfortunately."

Cathleen sank back into her chair. "I really hate how logical you can be sometimes. But can't you at least admit that our scenario is *possible?*"

Kelly covered half her face with her hand. After a moment, she sighed. "There are a few things I can look into."

"Thank you."

"But please promise you'll leave the investigation to the police. I'm not sure how you found out about Max's investments. Frankly, I'm glad I don't know."

"We didn't do anything wrong."

Kelly appeared skeptical. "Just stay out of trouble. Okay?"

Cathleen thought about the plan she and Dylan had to visit Danny Mizzoni later that day. Kelly would definitely not approve. Still, it couldn't be helped. Max had to be stopped. That was the priority.

So Cathleen nodded, making a promise she knew she would break.

"HOW WELL DO YOU KNOW DANNY?" Dylan asked Cathleen as they drove toward the Thunder Bar M late that afternoon. His attention at the moment was divided among Cathleen, the road and the storm clouds piling in from the northwest.

"Only by reputation, really." Cathleen rolled up her window against the cooling wind. "I know his brother, Mick, better. He was in my grade at school. A quiet, serious kid who was always top of the class. And *good-looking,* let me tell you."

Dylan laughed. "Should I be jealous?"

"No. Mick never gave me a second glance. Or any of the other girls at school. We used to wonder if he was gay."

"He's the editor at the *Canmore Leader,* right?"

"And he owns a beautiful home, not far from where Max lives. Yeah, he's done well for himself, Mick Mizzoni. Nothing like the rest of his family. You've heard about their mother, and of course Danny's been trouble since the day he was born."

"He's quite a bit younger than Mick, isn't he?"

"About five years, I think. Which makes him around twenty-four."

"Any idea when he started getting in trouble?"

"Dylan, Danny was *always* in trouble. I'll never forget an incident that happened when he was just a kid, only six years old or so. He trashed Kelly's bike—hurled stones at it until it was mangled, then left it in our driveway. Maureen saw him do it."

"Imagine a little guy like that having so much anger. What was his daddy like?"

"I don't know. Isabel Mizzoni never married. Danny and Mick look so dissimilar everyone always assumed they had different fathers."

Dylan eased off the accelerator in anticipation of turning left. He took the approach road slowly, not wanting to kick up too much dirt or create too much noise. As the house came into view, the decrepit window coverings and the trash that littered the yard gave him a hollow, futile feeling.

"Goddammit..."

Cathleen put a hand on his knee. "It's okay, Dylan. We'll fix it up the way it used to be."

He stopped the truck and got out, hoping the kids would be having a nap or something. But one of the bedsheets over the window shifted, and he caught sight of two young faces, barely able to see over the sill.

A second later, the front door slammed.

"Dylan, what're you doing here?" Danny's jeans were dirty and his feet were bare. A black leather jacket, too heavy for the weather, hung unzipped from his shoulders. He put a hand out to the front porch railing, obviously needing help to keep his balance.

Dylan checked Cathleen's expression. She was grimacing, shaking her head. Danny was obviously drunk or stoned, maybe a little of both.

"Checking up on my property, Mizzoni." He kicked an aluminum beer can out of his path. "Can't say I'm too impressed with the landscaping."

"Well, you're not signing my paycheck," Danny pointed out. "But the man who is says you've got no business on this land."

Dylan took a few more steps, then paused. "I'm not going to hurt anything, Danny. Just wanted to ask you a few questions. Is that okay?" He put one booted foot on the first stair of the veranda. Above him, Danny appeared dazed.

"I need to sit." Danny slid down to the top step.

Cathleen came up from behind, brushing past

Dylan to settle next to Danny. Did she think she had to stay between them to prevent trouble? If so, she was mistaken. Dylan wasn't going to lay a hand on Danny. Not in his current condition. The man was an absolute mess. Dylan hoped he hadn't over-dosed on something.

"Can you tell me what you were doing last Tues-day night, Danny?"

The young man's eyes were too prominent in his gaunt face. Now they rolled in Dylan's direction, displaying a flash of intelligence. "That was the night your mother was killed."

"Yeah."

Danny glanced at the window. His wife's face was now visible, too, above those of the small chil-dren. He waved for them to go away, and they did. The sheet settled back over the window.

"I was here at home. Sharon will tell you it's true. We rented a movie. Drank a few beers, maybe smoked a few joints." He smiled weakly. "Didn't tell the cops about that last part, of course."

So the RCMP *had* questioned Danny. Knowing they weren't concentrating their investigation en-tirely on *him* made Dylan feel marginally better.

"And you never left the house?" Dylan asked.

"Not even for fifteen minutes."

Danny shook his head. "I told you no. Just ask Sharon."

Dylan caught Cathleen's skeptical gaze and

raised his eyebrows. As Danny's wife, Sharon wouldn't make the most impartial corroborating witness.

"How much money does Strongman pay you to look after this place?"

"None of your business, is it?"

"That's an awfully nice vehicle you have parked in the lane. Just wondering what we'd find if we checked your bank records. Any particularly big deposits lately, Danny?"

"I don't know what you're talking about." But the flush suffusing Danny's cheeks had a decidedly guilty cast to it.

Dylan felt a splash of water hit his hand, followed by the distinctive hollow sound of raindrops hitting the taut weave of his hat. A quick check of the sky confirmed that the gathering storm had arrived. Off in the distance, he heard the rumble of thunder.

Danny was scrambling to his feet. "Better get going," he told them. "Judging from them clouds, sky's about to crack open."

"But it's nice and dry up here on the veranda." Dylan climbed the extra steps necessary to put him under cover with Danny and Cathleen. "I've just got a few more questions, Danny. Like, if you really were home that night, maybe you'd already bought a gun for someone else to do the deed?"

Shakily, Danny moved for the front door. With two large strides, Dylan intercepted him.

"Tell me the truth, Danny." The younger man was just a few centimeters shorter than Dylan, but his physical condition was poor. Dylan's muscles were cords of steel; Danny's had atrophied on his skinny, almost malnourished frame.

Still, Danny bristled with desperate overconfidence. "I don't have to explain nothin' to you. I didn't do anything wrong—I never bought anyone a gun and I had that money coming to me from a long ways back."

Up close, Danny didn't smell any better than he looked. Dylan stepped backward as Cathleen practically forced her way between them.

"If you didn't do anything wrong, Danny, then why don't you want to help us? Finding Rose's murderer will get the cops off your back, as well as Dylan's."

"I ain't interested in helping nobody. Nobody's ever been too worried about helping me."

Danny tried to walk past the two of them for the door, but a sound from the drive stopped him.

Not thunder, the rumbling had come from an approaching vehicle, which was only now coming into view. Dylan was surprised to see the distinctive markings of an RCMP vehicle, but Danny was ignited.

"Jesus Murphy! You guys are in cahoots with them, aren't you."

Dylan needed a second to realize what he meant. "We had no idea," he began. But Danny was already in a lather.

"This is a bust, isn't it?" He grabbed for Cathleen, and caught her upper arm just as the police cruiser braked to a stop next to Dylan's truck.

Dylan panicked at the unexpected maneuver. "Leave her alone, Danny."

"Like hell I will." Danny yanked Cathleen's arm behind her back, positioning her like a shield against the world.

"Let go, you idiot!" Cathleen kicked Danny in the shin with the heel of her boot just as Dylan went for the man's throat.

From the depths of his black coat, Danny pulled out a revolver. Pointing the muzzle at Cathleen's chest, he jerked his head toward Dylan.

"Back off, McLean. I guess you'll listen to me now."

CHAPTER THIRTEEN

WITH THE OLD-MODEL Smith & Wesson in his hand, Danny became a different person. Cool, brash, confident.

"You think you're such a hotshot," he said to Dylan, "but your daddy gave you everything. You don't know what it's like to start off in this world with nothin'. And I mean *nothin'*. Not even your old man's last name to show the world what you're made of."

Fear tasted bitter in Dylan's mouth. That gun was pointed at the person in this world who mattered most to him. And Mizzoni was way more unstable than he'd guessed.

"Danny, put your gun away. This is crazy, man. We just came here to talk."

A car door sounded behind him, but Dylan didn't dare take his eyes off Danny to check which RCMP officer had arrived. The clouds had darkened the sky, giving the illusion of dusk. Still, enough light filtered through for him to see Cathleen's pale face grow whiter.

"Danny, you're hurting my arm," she said.

Her voice sounded mildly annoyed, no trace of the terror she had to be feeling. Dylan realized she was trying to distract Danny from the approaching cop.

"And you know you don't want to shoot me," she added.

"We only wanted your help," Dylan added softly. "We never meant you any harm by coming here."

"Oh yeah? Then explain *her!*" Danny glanced over at the cop, and now Dylan looked, too.

Lord. It was Kelly. Advancing through the streaming rain, her Smith & Wesson semiautomatic secure in her right hand.

"Police. Drop the gun, Danny," she said. She meant to sound tough, Dylan was sure, but her voice trembled and her gaze shifted nervously toward Cathleen.

"Stop right there!" Danny ordered. "Or I'll shoot her—I swear I will!"

Kelly stopped. Dylan squeezed his fists in agony. He longed to lunge for the gun in Danny's hand...but what if it was loaded and ready to fire? He might be too slow; he couldn't take that chance.

"Danny, you don't want to go to jail. You've got a wife and two kids. A good job." Kelly's words were reasonable, her tone soothing, as she carefully dared another step.

"Don't move!" With his thumb, Danny cocked

the hammer of his handgun, leaving no doubt as to his intention. Cathleen gasped at the sound, lost her balance and fell forward.

Danny panicked at the unexpected movement. "I said *don't move!*"

Cathleen froze. "Jeez, Danny, I'm sorry. I tripped, all right?"

"It's okay, Danny," Dylan said, using his most soothing, horse-settling voice. "Everything's okay...."

The young man's panting was audible as he swung his head from Dylan to Kelly, then back again. Dylan could see the coating of sweat on Danny's forehead; in fact, he was damn sure he could smell it, too.

Again, he was reminded of a young horse in training. The fear, the distrust, the desperate need to escape.

"That's it. Take it easy," he murmured.

Uncertainty widened Danny's eyes. The hand holding the gun lowered an inch. *Yes! He was coming to his senses!*

And then, with terrible timing, a clap of thunder rolled down from the mountains, echoing against the valley walls.

Danny's gun jerked in his hand and Cathleen screamed. With horror, Dylan realized the frightened man was adjusting his aim, was about to fire—

An explosion sounded, and Danny fell backward.

Cathleen put a hand to her chest, as if searching for a bullet wound. But it was Danny who'd been shot. Dylan could see the blood seeping around the hole in the black jacket. A moment later the gun fell from Danny's hand.

"My God…" Kelly ran forward. "My God… Is he still breathing?"

Dylan didn't know, and didn't much care at the moment. He reached for Cathleen, pulling her away from Danny, pressing her tightly against his chest. For a split second, he'd thought he'd lost her. Thank God for her sister's accurate aim.

Kelly knelt beside the stricken man and gently checked for a pulse. Just then the front door flew open.

"What the f—" The profanity froze on Sharon's lips when she saw the prone figure of her husband, the blood on the porch and Kelly's desperate attempts to stop the bleeding. The couple's two children peered out from behind her legs. Sharon covered their faces with trembling hands, her eyes still trapped by the site of her unmoving husband.

Gently, Dylan lowered Cathleen to the floor, urging her to rest her head against her bent knees. Then he went to Danny. A quick assessment brought a blunt verdict: no breathing, no heart rate.

Kelly pressed her jacket to Danny's wounds, whispering, "No, Danny, no!"

"It's too late," he said softly, crouching beside

her. He could hear the rain, rattling like machine-gun fire against the cedar shingles of the porch roof. Kelly's hair was wet and flattened—somehow she'd lost her hat.

"Backup is on the way," she said, her tone desperate. "They'll take him to the hospital...."

"It's too late," he repeated. "He had a gun on Cathleen. I'm sure he was about to pull the trigger. You did what you had to do. Now, come over here and rest until help arrives."

"Don't touch anything," Kelly said urgently. "Especially not Danny's gun..."

"I understand. Don't worry." This was a crime scene now. He took her to Cathleen, who opened her arms.

"Kelly...you saved my life."

"Did he hurt you?"

"N-no. I'm fine."

Finally, Dylan turned to Danny's family. Like three statues, the mother and her children remained at the threshold, neither inside the house nor out on the porch. Dylan moved to block their gruesome view just as Kelly noticed them, too.

"I'm so sorry." Her knees gave out and she reached for one of the pillars that had helped to steady Danny just minutes ago. "I'm just so sorry."

The little girl started to cry. Danny's wife dropped to her knees and held the child's face to her chest. The young boy noticed none of this. Just stared at his father, at the pool of blood gathering on the porch floor.

"It's going to be okay." Dylan picked up the little guy. He didn't resist, but his body remained stiff. "Let's go to the kitchen." He nudged Sharon forward, then glanced back at Cathleen and Kelly.

"Maybe you two should sit in my truck until the ambulance arrives," he suggested. Cathleen nodded gratefully.

Inside, the ranch home was dark. Sheets covering the windows kept out what little light was leaking past all those storm clouds. Dylan walked through clutter and dirt, leading the stricken family to the kitchen at the back. He found remnants of past meals scattered on the counter and the old oak table. The same table that had been at the center of so many of his happiest old memories.

Dylan set the small boy in a chair, then reached a hand to Sharon's shoulder. "What can I do to help? Is there someone I should call?"

For the first time, a spark showed in Sharon's eyes. "Danny's brother, Mick. He works at the paper."

"Sure." The same black phone still hung on the wall by the table. Dylan checked with Information, then dialed the number to the *Canmore Leader*. Eventually someone gave him Mick's cell phone number. By a stroke of luck, Mick had just gotten into his car on the way to Calgary.

"I'm turning around right now," he said. "Tell Sharon I'll be five minutes, tops." He paused a moment. "Help her with Billy and Mandy until I arrive, okay?"

"Of course." Dylan hung up, not sure what he'd agreed to do. How in the world was he going to help these poor kids? Mandy clung to her mother's shoulder, still crying. Billy sat like an obedient pupil, his hands folded on the sticky kitchen table, his feet swinging underneath him.

"Anybody need a drink?"

Sharon's eyes snapped to the fridge. "Get me a beer...."

"Sure thing." He found an aluminum can and assumed Sharon wouldn't worry about transferring the liquid to a glass. No sooner had he popped the tab than Sharon took the can from him and poured half the contents down her throat.

"What about you, Billy? Thirsty?"

Billy shook his head in the negative. He watched his mother pace the room, one arm wrapped under Mandy's bottom, the other clutching the drink Dylan had given her.

Dylan wondered if the little girl would come to him and give her mother a break. But predictably, when he held out his hands her wails just got louder.

Then Billy slid off his chair. He went to his

mother and tugged on Mandy's leg. "Come on, Amanda. I'll hold you."

Magically, the little girl's tears stopped. She slid down her mother as though Sharon were a fireman's pole. Sharon didn't seem to notice as her little son took Mandy's hand and led her to a corner. Watching the children cuddle like two cold puppies, Dylan couldn't hold back a couple of tears.

The faint wail of sirens was just becoming audible when Cathleen appeared at the back door with Kelly behind her. "Mick Mizzoni just showed up. Is everything okay? The emergency vehicles sound like they're almost here."

"Yeah. I hear them."

Cathleen's gaze fell on the children. "Oh, Dylan!" She spoke softly, but the pain in her voice echoed what he'd been feeling.

"I know." He was reaching out to hold her when footsteps echoing in the large, underfurnished rooms out front announced Mick Mizzoni's approach.

"Sharon? Billy?" An exceptionally good-looking man paused at the entranceway to the kitchen, his expression one of shock. He pulled a hand through his thick, longish brown hair and shook his head slightly.

"Uncle Mick!" Billy ran to the newcomer, dragging his sister along.

It was hard to believe this man could be Danny's

brother. There was precious little resemblance between them. Mick dropped to one knee and embraced both children tightly. "Are you guys okay?"

For the first time since his father had been shot, Billy started to cry.

Dylan watched, feeling uncharacteristically helpless as the man did his best to comfort the small children. After a few minutes, Mick glanced at his sister-in-law.

"Sharon? You all right?"

Silent tears had taken their toll on the thin blonde. She nodded, holding the beer can close to her chest. "That lady cop shot Danny. Just shot him, like he was an animal."

Mick's gaze flicked dismissively past Dylan and Cathleen, who still stood at the doorway. Into the silence stepped Kelly, pushing past her sister's protective stance.

"Kelly Shannon?" Mick shook his head slowly. "No. Not you."

Tears welled in Kelly's eyes, but she sounded composed as she answered. "Yes, it's true. I'm so sorry, Mick...."

"She shot Danny," Sharon said again, pointing her finger right at Kelly's chest. "She killed him."

Kelly flinched but didn't back down. Dylan admired her strength as she squared her shoulders and turned to meet the emergency vehicles now streaming into the ranch yard—a couple of squad cars and an ambulance. The sight brought back terrible, haunting memories from two years ago when there'd been another shooting death on this ranch.

Was this place cursed? Or was it him?

DANNY MIZZONI WAS DEAD and it had happened right before Cathleen's eyes. She wished she could block out the memory, but she knew she never would. Even down here, by the creek with Dylan, she could still picture the bloody porch and Danny lying twisted and lifeless.

Dead. It didn't seem possible, but it was the truth. Danny Mizzoni, who was not a model citizen, who was in all likelihood a murderer, might have seemed a small loss if she'd read about his death in a newspaper.

But she'd seen him shot down, and it had been horrible. All the more so because his wife and children were there. Cathleen kept remembering the way Mandy had scrambled into her daddy's arms the other day when she and Dylan had come to the ranch.

A little girl didn't run into arms she didn't trust. So Danny must've been okay as a father. Which meant Cathleen couldn't see him as a monster. He was a person, a husband, a daddy. And now he was dead, and she struggled to make sense of it all.

The violent storm had passed earlier, while they

were giving their statements to Sergeant Springer. Faint rumblings of thunder occasionally sounded from farther down the valley, but the rain had eased off and the clouds were lifting.

"Danny must've had something to do with your mother's death, Dylan. Why else would he have gone for his gun like that?"

"Stupidity, probably." With a flick of his wrist, Dylan fired a stone at the surface of the slowly moving water. One, twice, three times the rock skipped before finally sinking under.

"Those poor children, seeing their father..." Cathleen, perched on a flat rock near the edge of the creek, buried her face in her hands. Having already given their statements to Staff Sergeant Springer, she and Dylan were waiting for Kelly.

Her sister had crumbled when help arrived—it was clear she was suffering from shock. Yet when Cathleen would have whisked her home, Thad had insisted she needed to be debriefed.

A splash drew Cathleen's attention back to the water. Dylan was volleying stone after stone. The water rippled as if rain were pelting it.

"What are you doing, Dylan? Trying to build a dam?"

He just swore and grabbed another handful of pebbles.

She was pretty sure where all the anger stemmed from. He blamed himself for what had happened.

Not that it made any sense for him to do so. He'd handled the situation with compassion and intelligence. For a moment there, he'd almost had Danny calmed down. Then that stupid clash of thunder had wrecked everything.

After the shooting, Kelly had started crying. She'd been so weak she couldn't even stand, but he'd kept his cool. He'd taken care of her and Kelly, protected the crime scene and handled Sharon and her kids.

Now he seemed to be suffering a delayed reaction to the stress. She could see his hands shake slightly as he launched yet another projectile into the water.

"Dylan, it isn't your fault Danny pulled that gun on me. No one could've guessed."

"Why not? We knew he was a criminal. We suspected he'd been involved in my mother's death. I should've at least considered the possibility that he could be dangerous."

"And why is that? Because you're a mind reader?"

"No, I'm a bloody fool who should've kept you out of this. When you were in Canmore with your sister, that's when I should've gone to talk to Danny."

"You make me so angry when you say stuff like that, I have to wonder if you have the foggiest clue what kind of person I am."

Dylan dropped his hands to his sides. "You're the most incredible, brave, loyal woman I've ever met. Most people would be scared witless with a crazy man pointing a gun at them. But you didn't give an inch. Cath, your backbone must be steel."

She opened her mouth to say more, closed it, then shook her head. How could she stay mad if he was going to retaliate with compliments?

"You know what the worst of this is?" Dylan said.

She couldn't ask. The situation seemed bad enough to her as it was.

"Danny probably panicked at the sight of that squad car because he thought he was getting caught in a drug raid. What do you want to bet the police find a stash of illegal substances when they search the ranch house?"

"Maybe so. But that doesn't mean he didn't kill Rose, too."

"Maybe."

"You don't sound very confident." If Danny wasn't involved in murder, that would make what had just happened all the harder to come to terms with. Not just for her and Dylan, but especially for Kelly.

He sighed and turned away from the creek. "Danny was just a small-time crook."

"He didn't seem so small-time when he had that gun pointed at my heart!"

"Oh, darlin'." Dylan came over and crushed her against his chest.

"He's the guilty one," Cathleen repeated. "He has to be."

"Well, we'll know soon enough." Dylan glanced toward the ranch house, where the police were still gathering evidence. "When they send that gun in for testing, they'll find out if it shot the bullet that killed my mother."

"And if it did, your name will be cleared."

"And if it didn't, a murderer will still be on the loose. And two kids will have lost a father for nothing." Dylan tossed a final stone into the river. "Come on, let's check out what's happening with Kelly."

CATHLEEN AND DYLAN FOUND Kelly leaning against her squad car. A female RCMP officer stood beside her. Several more official vehicles were on the scene now and uniformed men and women tramped the rain-drenched yard, taking photographs, collecting evidence, writing notes.

"Cathleen, Dylan, this is Corporal Webster," Kelly said. "She's from the Member Assistance Program in Calgary."

"What's going on?" Cathleen felt overwhelmed by all the people and activity.

"Backup arrived from Calgary. Ident and the Major Crimes Unit," Corporal Webster explained.

"Standard procedure for a situation like this. My job is to take care of Kelly and make sure she understands what'll happen to her."

"What *is* going to happen?" Cathleen asked, scared for her sister. She reached for Kelly's hand and found it cold and slack.

"She'll be suspended from duty with pay while we carry on an investigation."

Cathleen looked over at her sister. Lord, Kelly appeared ready to faint. "I'm taking her home."

"Sorry. We need her to go to the detachment first. As much for her protection as anything. She can call you when we're finished."

"Go on home," Kelly said. "I'll be okay."

"You'll phone when you're done? I don't want you going back to your apartment. You can stay with me for a few days." Cathleen gave her sister one last hug, then noticed Thad watching Dylan, a dark expression compressing his even features. Clearly he was drawing the worst possible conclusion from finding his number one suspect for Rose Strongman's death on the scene of yet another shooting. The whole scenario made Cathleen very nervous.

"Let's go, Dylan." She grabbed his arm and tugged, but Dylan resisted. Thad's expression grew even grimmer.

"You and trouble seem to have a standing date," the sergeant said to Dylan. Then he turned to Cathleen. "I wish I could understand what you see in him."

Cathleen paused, surprised by the bitterness in Thad's words. The two of them had dated, but never to an extent that would justify his acting like a jealous boyfriend. Which was exactly how he struck her right now.

"Thad, Dylan is innocent." Beside her, Dylan let out a muffled groan, which she ignored. "He *is*. I think Max Strongman may have hired Danny to kill Rose...." She lowered her voice. "Thad, you've got to check into this."

The sergeant shook his head. "He really has your number, doesn't he?"

He wasn't taking her seriously. Frustrated, she grasped his shoulder. "I'm telling you something important. If you would only investigate, you might see that I'm right."

Thad took a step closer to her, then brushed her hair back with his hand and lowered his mouth to within inches of her ear.

"Oh, I'm going to investigate, all right," he whispered. "But I'm willing to bet the evidence points right back at your boyfriend. Dump him, Cathleen. Before it's too late."

CHAPTER FOURTEEN

CATHLEEN DIDN'T FEEL LIKE talking on the drive back to the B and B, and Dylan obviously felt the same. She was worried about him as they trudged inside to fill Poppy in on the latest disaster. Of course she downplayed, as much as possible, the part where Danny had stabbed her ribs with his gun.

"Are you sure you're okay?" Poppy's face had turned white.

"Physically, I'm fine. Not even a bruise." Cathleen patted the hand Poppy placed on her shoulder. The damage to all of them—particularly Kelly—was more psychological.

"Chicken soup," Poppy prescribed. "I have some frozen stock...." She pulled a plastic container from the freezer, then a handful of fresh vegetables from the fridge door below.

Although doubtful that food of any type could help the situation, Cathleen thought it sweet of Poppy to make the effort. "I want Kelly to stay here for a few days. I'm going to prepare a room for her."

"I'll help," Dylan said, following.

At the top of the stairs, she pulled a stack of fresh-scented sheets from the linen cupboard and handed them to Dylan.

"I'm going to put her in here—" Cathleen opened the door to the room next to her own "—the Teddy Bear Suite." She'd had so much fun shopping for the bears that practically overflowed in this room. A shelf over the bed held a collection of small costumed bears. On the bed itself were several plushy Gunds. And two eighteen-inch bears in Victorian dresses sat at a small wicker table, an adorable miniature tea set spread out in front of them by the cushioned window seat.

"Wow." Dylan took in the vast array of collectibles. "This would be a little girl's idea of paradise."

Cathleen nodded. "Toss the sheets on that chair for now. I'll open the window."

She'd had a little girl in mind when she'd done this room, all right. The little girl she'd hoped to one day have with Dylan. Last time she'd seen James, he'd asked if she wanted kids. But the only man she'd ever wanted children with was Dylan. Undoubtedly they'd be little hellions, but they'd be darlings, too.

She and Dylan had planned on two children. They'd had so many dreams! First, this B and B, then a family they'd hoped to raise on the Thunder Bar M one day.

Some dreams, she acknowledged as she cracked open the window to freshen the room, died off a little slower than others. Accepting that those children she'd anticipated so keenly would never be born was still so hard.

"I'd say the sergeant has a major case of the hots for you," Dylan said, coming up from behind her. "You told me the two of you dated. But just how serious were you?"

She knew what he really was asking. She swiveled from the window to face him. "We never slept together."

Dylan's jaw relaxed.

"We didn't even go out that much. Thad is one of those guys who tries too hard. No matter what I was wearing, I was beautiful. No matter what I said, it was either funny or profound. He made me uncomfortable."

And never more so than this afternoon. She'd hated the familiar way he'd touched her hair, and that parting warning had been over the top.

Dylan slipped his arms around her waist and pulled her close. "The guy always acted like there was something personal between us. At least now I know what it is."

"You don't think…" She lifted her head to make eye contact. Dylan's expression was grim.

"That he's jealous? Damn right he is. Unfortunately for me, that gives him all the more reason for wanting me behind bars.''

"But—'' She thought back to the day Springer had been transferred to this town. How long ago was that? Maybe three years? She'd been engaged to Dylan by then but had met Thad a few times through Kelly. Then, once her wedding was canceled and Dylan had left, Thad was among the first to ask her out.

"We're talking about a murder investigation here, Dylan. He wouldn't let his feelings for me bias something so important.''

"What makes you so sure?''

"He's an RCMP officer. I guess I think they're all as honorable as Kelly. Sometimes she drives me *crazy,* she's so conscientious.''

Dylan's mouth twisted. "I wish we could count on Thad being the same. But that man has always seemed out to get me. You weren't there when I gave my statement, but he did his best to trip me up. He implied that I was trying to bully Danny and his family off the ranch.''

"That weasel.''

"You want to hear something weird? Knowing how he feels about you, I'm almost sorry for him. Losing you would make me go a little crazy, too....''

Dylan's arms tightened and he rested his chin on the top of her head. His embrace offered warmth, security, protection. But in reality he had none of those to give. Just as she could make no promises to him about his future.

WHEN CATHLEEN CAME DOWN to the kitchen Friday morning, two days after the shooting on the Bar M, Poppy was removing a blueberry bundt cake from the oven and the coffee smelled freshly brewed.

Cathleen watched as Poppy eased a wooden spatula around the cake, releasing it from the pan. Next, she inverted the pan over a pretty glass plate and out popped a golden-brown cake, topped with chopped nuts and deep-purple berries.

"That looks beautiful, Poppy."

"Kelly told me she liked blueberries. Have you noticed she's barely eaten since the shooting?" Poppy's assessing glance took in Cathleen's own anxious state. Abandoning her baking, she pulled a ceramic mug from the cupboard, filled it with coffee and passed it to Cathleen. "Here, you look like you need this."

"Thanks." Cathleen took a sip. Almost immediately, her stomach rebelled.

She'd had precious little sleep last night, and neither had Dylan. They'd held each other till dawn, talking about old times, trying to divert their thoughts from the main question that hung in their minds. Kelly was pretty sure the RCMP would get the results of the ballistics tests today. Then they'd know for sure whether Danny had killed Rose.

Absentmindedly, Cathleen picked at the crumbs on the counter.

"Would you like a slice?" Poppy asked.

"Maybe later. The cake smells delicious."

"I hope Kelly thinks so."

Reminded once more of her sister, Cathleen felt guilty for focusing on her own problems and Dylan's. Poppy was right. Kelly was on the edge, hardly eating or sleeping. Maureen had zipped out for a quick visit last night, but she had been unable to stay long. She was in court this week—an ugly divorce case where the parents were using money to battle for the kids. "I should run up and check on her."

Poppy stopped her with a touch on her arm. "I peeked in a few minutes ago and she was out like a light. Let her rest."

"All right." As Cathleen started in on the dishes, she reflected on how much she'd come to take Poppy's comforting presence for granted. "With all that's been going on lately, I'm surprised you don't pack up your bags and move out of here."

"Oh, I could never do that!" Poppy sounded as shocked as if Cathleen had suggested she empty the B and B checking account.

"Why not? It must be hard to concentrate on

your book when you've got murders and shootings going on all around you.''

"I get a surprising amount done in my room. The Internet is so helpful, especially for tracing my family tree. I've followed one branch all the way to the 1700s. Guess what? I'm seventh cousin once removed to the president of the United States.''

"George W. Bush?"

Poppy smiled. "It sounds silly, but I get a tremendous satisfaction from the process. It's a little like detective work really.''

"Is anyone else in your family interested in genealogy?"

Poppy's gaze dropped to the floor. "Not much family left these days. I've a few cousins and one brother. We were never close.''

There it was again, the feeling that Poppy didn't want to talk about her personal life. Still, Cathleen just couldn't curb her curiosity. "Were you never married, Poppy?''

"A long time ago. It didn't work out...."

"Any children?"

Poppy pressed her lips together and shook her head. "I can't—"

"I'm sorry." Cathleen felt guilty for asking questions she'd known weren't welcome. "I shouldn't have upset you. The truth is I'm feeling bad about our agreement. You're paying good money to stay here, but I'm not providing the peace and quiet you need. I'd be happy to refund the balance of your money if you want to find someplace else." It would hurt, given how slow business had been. But she would definitely find a way.

Poppy straightened and smiled, her composure regained. "Don't be silly. I'm here and I'm staying. Unless I've been getting in the way...?"

Cathleen threw a soapy hand around her boarder's shoulders. "Of course not. You're the *perfect* guest. As far as I'm concerned, you can stay *forever* if you want."

"Oh, Cathleen." Poppy squeezed her hand. "You and your sisters are such special people. I imagine your mother must have been very proud of you."

"She always said she was. I like to think she meant it."

Poppy's smile was tender. "You miss her."

Cathleen nodded. "Uh-huh. And I always will." Their mother had had the gift of connecting with each of her children. For her, it had been through their shared love of horses and the outdoors. Most of their best conversations had occurred while they were out riding.

"Is there anyone else in your family, besides your sisters, whom you're close to?"

"Not really. Like you, we never had a big family. Mom's sister married an Australian. We've never even met our cousins."

"What about your father's side of the family?"

Cathleen paused to think. "Mom never talked about them. I don't think she'd ever met her in-laws. They weren't from around here."

"You've never had any desire to track them down?"

Was Poppy thinking of offering her genealogy services?

"None. Unlike you, I have no interest in my family tree." Cathleen turned back to the sink, where she ran the beaters from the Mixmaster under a stream of hot water, clearing out the soap bubbles from the blades. "We're fine on our own. We never needed them, just as we didn't need our father."

"But didn't you ever miss him?" Kelly was speaking. She stood in the arched passageway that led from the stairs to the kitchen. Several inches of her skinny waist were revealed between the gray boxer shorts that rested on her hips and the short white tank top that she used for pajamas. Her hair was uncombed and dark circles defined her eyes. Cathleen felt a pang of concern.

"Did I wake you?"

"No." Kelly peered under the cloth Poppy had placed over the cake. "This smells good."

"Want a piece?" Poppy sounded so hopeful Cathleen felt badly for her when Kelly refused.

"Maybe later," she said. "I'm planning to drive to Calgary for the day. I've got an appointment with my lawyer, and Maureen wants me to go to lunch with her.''

''What about seeing a therapist, too?'' Cathleen asked. Maureen had suggested it last night, and to Cathleen it made sense. Dealing with what had happened at the Thunder Bar M was going to take a little time. The more opportunities Kelly had to work everything out in her mind, the better.

''I don't know....''

''Come on, Kelly. You can't go on like this. Something has to give. Why not try counseling? Maureen said she could recommend someone.''

''The people at Member Assistance have a list I can choose from. If I decide to go...''

Her sister's indecision tore at Cathleen's heart. Poor Kelly was suffering so much. If only children hadn't been involved; it might not have been so hard. ''You had no choice in what you did,'' she told her sister, as she'd been telling her for the past two-and-a-half days.

''There's always a choice. Although if I hadn't fired at Danny and he'd hurt you, I would never have forgiven myself for that, either.''

''So you did the right thing.''

But Kelly couldn't admit it. She glanced at the time on the microwave, then sighed. ''If I'm going to make that appointment, I'd better get in the shower.''

Once she was gone, Poppy and Cathleen shared a dispirited look.

"Poor thing, she's taking this so hard," Poppy said.

"I feel terrible that it happened because she was protecting *me*. Really, it was such a calamity of errors when you think of it. If Danny hadn't panicked and reached for that gun in the first place." Or if she and Dylan had been more careful, or Kelly hadn't followed them to the ranch, guessing from their conversation at the café what her sister might be up to. *If, if, if...*

Dishes done, Cathleen released the water from the sink, feeling at odds. Her heart ached for Kelly, but it seemed there was nothing she could do to help her sister come to terms with the shooting. Nothing she could do to help Dylan, either.

"I'll strip the beds and get the laundry started," she told Poppy. "Okay if I do your room, as well?"

"Love, I've told you a hundred times, I'm happy to wash my own bedding."

"Now, Poppy, you've already taken over the kitchen. You can't have the laundry room, too."

Dylan's room was immaculate when she entered to get his sheets. He hadn't slept in there for almost a week now. It was past time she prepared the room for future guests. Not that she could likely expect any very soon.

By the time she'd moved on to her own suite,

Dylan was in the shower. Cathleen stripped the queen-size bed, then proceeded to Poppy's room. When she had all the linens, she took them to the basement and put in the first load.

Returning upstairs, she found Dylan and Kelly in the kitchen, sampling Poppy's cake.

"Want a piece now?" Poppy asked.

"It's excellent," Dylan enthused. He was in jeans and a white T-shirt, his feet bare, his face freshly shaven. She wanted to run a hand down his smooth cheek and kiss that wonderfully sexy mouth.

But she felt self-conscious in front of Kelly and Poppy. Lavishing her attention on the bundt cake was probably safer.

As she reached for a clean plate, the phone rang. Since she was closest, she picked up the receiver. "Hello?"

"Cathleen. How are you today?"

She stiffened at the sound of the familiar voice. "I'm fine, Thad." Her gaze slid to Dylan. She watched him swallow his food, then take a gulp of coffee, never raising his eyes to her. "What's up? Did you want to speak with Kelly?"

"Yes, please."

Cathleen handed the phone to her sister and then sat by Dylan. She put a hand on his forearm, and felt how tense his muscles were. On the phone, Kelly was saying only "Yes, sir" and "No, sir," so drawing any conclusions about what was being said was hard.

As soon as Kelly hung up, Cathleen had to ask. "Did they get the ballistics reports?"

Kelly nodded. She was so pale Cathleen was afraid she might collapse. Apparently Dylan thought so, too, because he got up and helped her to a chair.

"Bad news?" he asked quietly. As if he'd been expecting this, as if he knew what Kelly was going to say before she managed to get out the words.

"The ballistics reports are in. The bullets didn't match." Kelly recited the facts woodenly before stating the obvious. "I guess Danny didn't shoot Rose after all."

CATHLEEN WINCED AND CLOSED her eyes. Kelly shook her head, then dropped it on her arms to the table. Even Poppy, who'd been standing at the sink rinsing dishes, sagged a little.

Dylan observed their reactions with a curious feeling of detachment. It was as if an invisible barrier had suddenly separated him from the rest of the world, so much so that when he spoke he almost didn't expect anyone would hear him.

"I figured I was wrong the minute I saw Danny step out on that porch so stoned he could hardly stand. I knew he didn't do it. Danny Mizzoni was too small-time for a crime like this."

"Why?" Kelly moaned. "I *needed* him to be guilty. I *killed* him…oh, God…"

Cathleen was immediately up in arms. "Danny Mizzoni was hardly an innocent man. Don't forget he pulled that gun on me, and I know he intended to shoot it, too. You saved my life."

Poppy moved protectively to Kelly's side. "What happens now, love? Will you be able to go back to work?"

"Not for a long time. After the criminal investigation, which could take months, the attorney general will decide whether I'll be charged or not. Assuming charges aren't laid, both the RCMP and the province will conduct an inquiry." She took a shaky breath. "Even if everything proceeds smoothly, it'll take a minimum of half a year. I can't bear to consider what'll happen if they *do* decide to lay charges."

"Oh, they won't!" Cathleen said. "They couldn't!"

Dylan hoped she was right. But he could tell Kelly's job wasn't her main concern right now. Cathleen's little sister had to live with the fact that she'd killed a man. And he had to live with the fact that she'd done it only because of his stupidity.

"Was there any other news?" Cathleen asked. "I don't understand why Danny would've freaked out like that if he was innocent."

"Depends what you mean by innocent." Kelly

brushed back her hair with her hands as she took a calming breath. "They found drugs in the loft of one of the barns. A significant quantity of marijuana and ecstasy and even some crack, which we didn't even know Danny was dealing. But that's not the most interesting thing."

All three of them were silent, waiting.

"While the staff sergeant was doing up the paperwork he asked about the new Land Rover."

Dylan nodded at Cathleen's glance.

"Sharon explained that Danny got the money from Max Strongman."

"See!" Cathleen said triumphantly. "Didn't we tell you?"

"Not as payment for shooting Rose or even procuring an illegal weapon," Kelly said quickly. "But for something almost as bizarre. Danny is Max's son."

"No." Dylan couldn't believe it.

"It's true. Apparently when Max was working in Canmore about twenty-five years ago, he hired Danny's mother's services a few times. When he was running for mayor, Danny spotted a resemblance in the photo on the campaign poster to a picture his mother had once given him. He confronted Max, who offered him money to keep quiet. I guess Strongman decided that being linked to one of the town bad boys wouldn't be good for his electoral image."

"Now, doesn't that sound like Max." Dylan gripped the edges of the kitchen sink and stared out the window at his land. Tanya Strongman had told them that Max had been unfaithful. But to think that he had fathered one of the Mizzoni boys.

"That *is* bizarre," Cathleen finally said. "Does Mick know?"

"According to the sergeant, nobody knew but Sharon and Danny. That was the condition under which Max gave them the money. But after today the news will be out. Sharon's determined that Max Strongman pay for his son's funeral and be acknowledged in the program as his father."

Danny's words came back to Dylan: *You don't know what it's like to start off in this world with nothin'...not even your old man's last name.* Danny was right. Dylan didn't know. But he was sure of one thing. Having Max Strongman for a father would be worse than having no father at all.

CHAPTER FIFTEEN

WHEN THEY HAD THE KITCHEN to themselves again, Cathleen made a suggestion.

"We need to talk to Beth Gibson once more. Max's alibi is the key to this whole thing. And she was definitely cagey the last time I saw her."

Dylan agreed. In fact, he'd planned to drive over to her real estate office in Canmore later this morning. But on his own.

"I don't see why we both need to go," he said. "You've started the laundry and you've probably got a list of other chores you've been putting off these past few weeks."

"So what? Clean sheets are important, but not quite on par with finding out who really killed your mom." Cathleen grabbed her keys from the hooks by the door. In her well-worn jeans and red T-shirt, she looked fresh and young and full of energy. Didn't anything ever get her down?

For Dylan, the news about Danny's gun had been surprisingly discouraging. Maybe he'd been hoping, more than he thought, that Danny actually *had* been involved. Of course, he still could have been. Possibly he'd used another gun and disposed of it after the crime. But how the hell would Dylan ever prove that?

"Look, Cathleen. That scene at Danny's took five years off my life. It would be better if I handled things myself from here on in."

"Oh, really?"

Her words were meek, but her eyes blazed fire. Lord. He wasn't sure if he could survive a dueling match with Cathleen right now. But he'd drawn his line in the sand; now he would have to defend it.

"I can't stand seeing you hurt." Physically, such as yesterday, or mentally, as she would be today when her old friends and neighbors shunned her company.

"But you said I handled myself well on Wednesday."

"You absolutely did."

"Then I fail to see why you wouldn't want me along today."

"It's not a question of *want*."

"Then what is it a question of? You said you don't want me hurt, but people *do* get hurt in life, Dylan, and you can't always protect them." She tilted her head a little, regarding him thoughtfully. "You have a thing about protecting women, don't you? Why didn't I see it before? First your mother. Now me."

"Is there something wrong with that?"

"There is if you're doing it for the wrong reasons. Dylan, maybe your mother was the kind of woman who was used to having a man look out for her. But I'm not."

His mother had been exactly that kind of woman. But he didn't see how that was relevant. Before he could make his point, however, Cathleen jabbed her keys in his direction and started talking again.

"I grew up in a household of women. We never needed a man to take care of us."

"I don't recall implying that you did."

"Dylan, every time you take responsibility for something bad that's happened to me—such as Danny pulling out that stupid gun—that's exactly what you're doing. Because you're not letting me take responsibility for myself."

Her logic was wrong. "You were only there because of me."

"I was there because of *me*. Because I love you, you damn fool."

He raised his voice to match hers. "Well, I love you, too. How do you suppose I'd feel if something happened to you?"

Cathleen threw her hands into the air. "You idiot. You just don't get it."

Was she trying to make him crazy on purpose? "What the hell are you talking about?"

"Why do you have the right to worry about what happens to me, but I don't have that same right where you're concerned? Dylan, you thought you were protecting me when you walked out on our wedding. In fact, you broke my heart.''

She meant it. What was more, she was right. Dylan felt a new aching in his chest. ''Cathleen, I never meant to hurt you.''

She put a hand to the screen door, started to push it open, then turned back to him. ''But that's all you'll ever do as long as you try to do what's best for me. When I need your help, I'll ask for it, and I know you won't let me down. Please let me do the same for you.''

He was at a loss for a reply. Somehow, with the best of intentions, he'd screwed things up pretty badly between them. He'd never meant to be condescending. He'd always respected Cathleen and considered her an equal.

So why hadn't he treated her that way?

''Okay, then,'' he said briskly. ''Let's go talk to Beth. Your car or mine?''

''Whatever,'' Cathleen said sweetly. ''I'm easy.''

DYLAN ENDING UP TAKING his truck. He drove to Beth Gibson's real estate office on Main Street and parked at a meter out front, just behind a navy Volvo. *Canmore's Alpine Realty.* On the sidewalk in front of the door he regarded the black lettering with doubt.

"This is a real long shot," he said.

"I know. But it's worth a try." Cathleen pushed against the handle. The door eased open a bit, then jammed. Beth stood at the small opening, blocking the way.

"Is this a business call?" the older woman asked stiffly.

"Not really," Cathleen replied. "We want to talk about Max Strongman and the night Rose was killed."

Beth's expression turned from unwelcoming to hostile. "I have nothing to say on either of those topics. Besides, I'm busy right now."

Dylan registered the hurt on Cathleen's face, which was quickly replaced with a stubborn determination.

"Beth, I don't want to make a scene. Just let us in and we can have a nice quiet chat."

"What, exactly, do you want to know?"

"Maybe you could start by telling us what your husband, Alan, makes of your relationship with the mayor?"

It was the right question. In a flash, Beth had them inside the office and was locking the door behind them. "Hush, Cathleen! You'd better be careful before you make insinuations like that. In a town of this size, it doesn't take much to start gossip flowing."

She was so flustered Dylan knew they'd touched

a nerve. Despite himself, he felt a flutter of excitement. Could Cathleen be right? If only they had one tiny supporting fact. Something to throw Beth totally off balance.

And then he remembered. He went back to the front window and took another look at the car parked in front of his truck. As he'd thought, it was a navy Volvo. Surely that couldn't be coincidence.

He turned back to face Beth. "The night of my mother's funeral your car was parked outside Strongman's house. You were the last to leave." Still there, in fact, after Danny's departure, although at the time Dylan had assumed the car belonged to one of the neighbors and that Danny was the final visitor.

Beth's eyes widened. "How did you…? Never mind. Max and I have worked together for many years. It was a condolence call."

"But all the mourners were gone. The two of you were alone. Did your husband know where you were?"

Her glance sidled to framed photographs on the counter. Two young men in graduation caps and capes. Her sons.

"Alan was with me," she said.

Beth was an honest woman. That explained why she lied so badly. Her face colored; her eyes shifted to the left. Nervously, she pushed the sleeves of her cashmere sweater up to her elbows, then pulled them back down again.

Dylan put his hand on a phone. "Should I call him and ask if he would verify that?"

Beth's hand automatically shot out to stop him. Their eyes met, and he saw shame flash over her features before she turned away.

"I may have been wrong.... Alan may have left a few hours earlier."

"We don't want to cause trouble between you and Alan," Cathleen said. "Please just answer our questions. Beth, the night Rose was shot, you were in a council meeting with Max. At around nine-thirty, you took a twenty-minute break. Are you sure Max didn't—"

"No!" Beth's hand went to the pearl necklace at her throat. She pulled it so tightly it was amazing the strand didn't break. "I've already told you he couldn't have gone home. We were together for the entire break. Except for two minutes when I went to the washroom. Surely you don't think he could've rushed home, shot Rose, then rushed back in two minutes."

Something wasn't right. Beth wasn't telling the truth, or if she was, not all of it. Dylan guessed that Cathleen had the same impression. Clearly unsatisfied with Beth's responses, she wouldn't give up.

"Are you absolutely certain you've got the right night, Beth? Please, think this over carefully. You don't want to make the mistake of protecting someone who could be very dangerous.''

Beth's pretty mouth twisted with disdain. "The idea of Max shooting Rose is absurd."

Dylan was incredulous. Was it love that had this woman blinded to Max's flaws? His superficial charm and his good looks were all too effective at winning over the ladies. Obviously she had a secret passion for the man. Or maybe they were actually having an affair.

"I don't believe you know Max Strongman as well as you think you do," he said, wanting to warn her for her own sake.

"Or maybe Cathleen doesn't know *you* as well as *she* thinks." Beth crossed her arms rigidly in front of her chest and faced the younger woman. "Instead of insulting me with all these questions, maybe you should be asking a few of yourself. We *know* Dylan was at his mother's house the night she was murdered. So how can you be so certain he didn't do it?"

The woman's unexpected attack froze Cathleen for a second. And in that instant, Dylan was reminded that his lover did have her doubts. No matter how much she tried to convince him—maybe even herself—that she didn't. The knowledge brought pain, even though he couldn't blame her.

Cathleen recovered quickly. "I *do* know Dylan is innocent."

"And I know the same about Max," the older woman countered. Her still-youthful eyes blazed with a passion that had Dylan suddenly afraid for her. She could be Max's third victim. He wondered if it would help if he told her about Tanya....

But Beth wasn't listening. "I'm not putting up with this for another second. Get out, both of you." This time *she* picked up the phone. "I'm calling 911 if you don't leave immediately."

OUT ON THE STREET, the sun blazed gloriously, indifferent to the tumultuous emotions of the people below. As Dylan slipped on his sunglasses, Cathleen noticed his hands were trembling.

"Let's grab something to eat," she suggested, even though she wasn't at all hungry. They ducked into a pizza joint a few doors down from Beth's real estate office. Once settled in a cozy corner booth, with a combination pizza and two colas ordered, she felt it was safe to talk.

"Beth and Max. There's definitely something going on there, don't you agree?"

"She's in love with him."

"I think so, too. But are they having an affair?"

"If not, they're on the cusp. Frankly, I just don't get it. Beth is attractive and intelligent. Why would she fall for a guy like Strongman?"

"That man has fooled a lot of women. He *can* be charming when he wants to be."

Dylan leaned back in his chair as the server brought their drinks in frosted glasses. After she left, he leaned forward again. ''So she's lying to protect him?''

''Absolutely. Did you notice she wouldn't give us any details about where they were or what they were doing during council break?''

''Well, if they slipped out somewhere for a quickie, I could see why she'd be a little vague on the particulars.''

Cathleen grimaced at the idea of them together in that way. ''You know, Beth could be protecting Max for other reasons. What if he was blackmailing her?''

''About what?''

''How would I know? It would have to be about something Beth wanted to keep secret.''

When the pizza arrived, they ate quickly, then Dylan signaled the server for their check. ''There are thousands of possibilities if we want to speculate. What we need is some good solid evidence.''

''Well, the RCMP don't seem to need any of that to accuse *you* of the crime,'' she pointed out.

After settling their account, they drove back to the B and B. When they arrived, a shiny black Land Rover was parked in the space reserved for Poppy's red Tracker.

''Oh, hell,'' Dylan muttered, eyeing Max Strongman's vehicle unhappily.

With no sign of their uninvited guest outside, Cathleen hurried toward the house, anticipating the worst. She rarely locked the B and B. Would Max have dared enter without permission?

Almost immediately, she saw that he had. As she came round to the side door, she almost bumped into Max and his son, James.

Max settled back on the heels of his boots and hitched his thumbs under the brown leather belt that held crisp Wrangler jeans on his narrow hips. A paunch about the size of a soccer ball obscured all but the lower edge of an ornate silver buckle.

Beside his tall, solid father, James appeared slight and almost insubstantial, even though he stood almost six feet. Father and son wore matching maroon gold shirts; a logo stamped in gold letters on the upper left side read Thunder Valley Developments.

"What in the world is going on…?"

Max held up a glass of water. "We just got here a minute ago. James needed to use the facilities and I helped myself to a drink. We knocked, but the door was unlatched."

"That's because generally I trust my neighbors not to poke around my house when I'm not in."

Max seemed truly offended. "We didn't poke. I hoped you wouldn't mind. We've always given you free range to ride your horse wherever you want on our property."

Our property. Cathleen could see Dylan's mouth tighten at Max's possessiveness. She realized this was the first time the two men had come in contact since Rose's death. Afraid of the possibilities, she laid a restraining hand on Dylan's arm. He was glaring at Strongman with a hatred that increased her fear.

"You didn't attend your mother's funeral," Max said. He took a step forward, extending a hand in a conciliatory gesture. Dylan held firm, his expression dismissive.

"I had my own ceremony," he said.

"Yeah. I saw the tree. Very nice. I ended up scattering her ashes around it. Thought she'd be happy there...."

Cathleen couldn't help but feel touched. She glanced at Dylan and saw Max's comment had caught him off guard. He nodded at his stepfather, opened his mouth to say something, then just swallowed.

"Look, Dylan, I'm sorry for the way things turned out between you and me."

The man sounded so sincere. If he was capable of this kind of acting, it was no surprise he had Beth Gibson convinced of his innocence. Cathleen hated to be cynical, but she wondered if he'd told the truth about scattering Rose's ashes.

"I know I've made mistakes," Max continued.

"But what happened to your mother...that wasn't my fault."

"Wouldn't you like us to believe that." Dylan's hands flexed at his side as he watched his stepfather with the intensity of a contestant in a boxing ring.

"Why shouldn't you? It's the truth." Max stood his ground against the younger man. "I doubt if you understand the situation as well as you think you do."

Dylan stepped forward. "While I was gone my mother aged fifteen years in the space of two."

"And who was to blame for that? She couldn't get over what you'd done to Jilly."

"You bastard. You tortured her with your lies, even though you knew I had nothing to do with hurting that girl." Every muscle in Dylan's body tightened. His reaction reminded her of a wild animal preparing to spring. Cathleen used both hands to circle the biceps of his right arm.

"Do I?" Max's tone was taunting, the sort of challenge designed to make Dylan lose his cool.

Sure enough, Dylan broke out of her hold and grabbed Max's shirtfront. As Max wrenched away, the fabric of his shirt tore. For the first time, the mayor's composure slipped. "Look what you've done, you dirty little—" He drew back his fist in anger.

"I'm a lot stronger and more experienced than the last time you beat the crap out of me. Throw that punch and I'll be glad to show you what I learned in my years on the rodeo circuit.''

Max cursed but backed off. During the exchange James must have sidled toward the Land Rover without Cathleen's noticing. Now she saw him swing open the passenger door from his position in the driver's seat.

"Let's go, Dad. There's no point in talking. They won't listen.''

Max straightened the collar of his shirt, then smoothed down his hair. "We came here to make you a more-than-fair offer, but since you're not interested…''

Cathleen wanted to turn her back on the man, but she was curious. "What offer?''

"To take this place off your hands. I've heard business has been slow….'' He glanced at Dylan, placing the blame where he was sure it belonged. "You're too young to be saddled with this kind of financial worry.''

"I don't want to sell the B and B.''

"We'd pay fair market value, plus a premium for the improvements you've made.''

Thunder Valley Development. The logo on Max's shirt, clearly legible above the tear Dylan had made around the collar, caught her eye, and suddenly the unexpected offer more than made sense. She realized she should've been expecting something like this since the day she'd broken off with James.

Clearly, her riverfront land had a lot of appeal for the Strongmans' and their development plans.

"Forget it."

Dylan pulled her close and whispered, "Maybe you should think about it."

"What?" She couldn't believe he would entertain, for one second, the prospect of her doing business with the Strongmans.

"I'm not selling," she reiterated.

Dylan pulled a little harder on her arm. Still speaking in a low voice, he said, "You could rake in a big pile of money. Enough to make a clean start—when this is over."

When this was over, there would be no happily ever after for her and Dylan. She knew better than to count on that, which was all the more reason for her to keep the B and B.

"If I ever *did* sell, it wouldn't be to *you*."

Max made a noise of disgust. "Girl, you are such a fool." He sank into the passenger seat of the Rover and James took off. Cathleen stood watching them, her stance broad, one hand up to shield her eyes from the sun.

"Those men make me sick. Anything for the almighty dollar."

Frowning, Dylan fixed his gaze on the lane. The dust still hadn't settled from the Land Rover's departure. Likewise, a disquieting thought hadn't stopped kicking around in his head.

"Sometimes you've got to be practical," he said. "Besides, what if I've been wrong about Max?"

"Pardon me?"

"Sorry. A really bizarre possibility occurred to me. I must be light-headed."

Cathleen stroked his arm. "It's been a tough day. Why don't you go down to the barn and take Cascade out for a run. She'd love the exercise and I need to take care of that laundry."

CHAPTER SIXTEEN

CATHLEEN LEFT DYLAN AND WENT inside. The quiet house didn't seem as welcoming as usual. Poppy had left a casserole in the oven and there were two notes on the table. The one from Poppy explained that she would be spending the weekend with Harvey at Emerald Lake Lodge.

Cathleen was glad the older woman was having a little fun. Lately she'd been concerned that Poppy was getting dragged into their problems—hers and Kelly's—too much. Harvey had arrived on the scene with perfect timing.

The second note, from her sister, Kelly, said she would be back for dinner but made no reference to where she'd gone or what she was doing.

Oh, Kelly. Please be okay.

Although she still wasn't hungry, Cathleen made a salad to accompany the casserole, and set the table. Then she went downstairs to shift the laundry from the washer to the dryer, only to discover that Poppy had already taken care of everything.

She traipsed back up the stairs, with Rose's kitty at her heels. The poor thing was lonely. Despite the fact that she *really* wasn't a cat person, Cathleen caved and scooped the animal into her arms. She carried her to the study and sat petting the soft white fur until she heard a vehicle drive up.

"Thanks, Crystal," she told the cat. "That was exactly what I needed."

She went back to the kitchen, where she met Kelly. Her sister's face was pale, her hair pulled back into a utilitarian ponytail.

"Dylan just rode up on Cascade," Kelly said. "He said to tell you he'd just be a minute."

Cathleen took stock of her sister's haggard expression. "Are you okay?"

"Not bad" was all Kelly would answer.

A moment later the screen door opened again. Dylan's cheeks were ruddy, but the ride hadn't done much for his mood. Silently he washed his hands at the kitchen sink, then they all sat down to stare at food none of them felt like eating.

To hear another vehicle pull into the drive was almost a relief. Cathleen hoped for a new guest. That would prove to everyone that Dylan's presence at the B and B wasn't hurting her business. She crossed the room to check out the arrival. And felt a jolt of panic at the sight of the white car pulling up behind Dylan's truck. This was no guest; it was the RCMP.

"WE HAVE A WARRANT," Sergeant Springer told Cathleen at the side door. Although he spoke to her, his gaze shot to Dylan, still sitting at the kitchen table. The hostility between the two men was palpable.

"I don't understand, Thad. What are you looking for?"

"Evidence, Cathleen." His expression softened measurably when his focus shifted to her. "I hate to barge in—I'm sure you know that. But this warrant gives us the right to search the premises."

She scanned the official document, then sighed and shook her head. "What do we do?"

"Nothing. Go ahead and finish eating, if you'd like."

As if any of them now had the slightest appetite! Cathleen peered at the court document again, then glanced over her shoulder at Kelly.

"Let him in," Kelly said. "He's just doing his job."

Springer nodded at Kelly, then made eye contact with Dylan again. Dylan showed no reaction, but the same loathing rose up in Springer's narrowed eyes.

Cathleen felt fear. He wasn't going to arrest Dylan, was he? There was no concrete evidence, other than the eyewitness who'd seen Dylan leave his mother's house that night.

"You know, Thad, I was speaking to Beth Gibson today and there's a real possibility that something's going on between her and Max Strongman.''

''Cathleen...'' Dylan's tone cautioned her to be quiet, but she couldn't. She had to convince the sergeant he'd been neglecting other possibilities in his investigation.

''I think that makes Max's alibi pretty unreliable, don't you?''

Springer appeared unimpressed. ''Excuse me, please, Cathleen. I need to get this over with. I'll start upstairs.''

''Oh, go ahead.'' It was probably Dylan's bedroom he was so interested in. Dispirited, she turned back to the kitchen table. Both Dylan and Kelly were staring at the plates in front of them.

''He isn't going to find anything,'' she said, not sure if she was trying to reassure them or herself. But less than ten minutes later, Springer was back, a triumphant smile curving his lips.

And in his hands, encased in a clean plastic bag, was a gun.

Cathleen stared at the weapon. Not a toy from Wal-Mart, but the real thing. The weight of it stretched the plastic bag out tight and long.

Springer looked as pleased as a magician who'd just produced a rabbit from inside a hat. ''I warned you not to trust him, Cathleen. He's taken advantage of you yet again.''

''I don't believe this.'' She rose from the table,

keeping a wary distance from the object in the bag. "You didn't find that here."

"I sure did. It's called a Saturday-night special—illegal in Canada, by the way. A .32 caliber, same type used to kill Rose Strongman. We'll have to confirm all this with ballistics testing, of course, but that won't take long."

"Where did you find it?" Kelly was the one to ask the burning question.

"Under the mattress in the room in the southeast corner."

Dylan's room. And Springer knew it. Cathleen couldn't breathe. That gun—why would Dylan own such a thing? She swung her head toward him and found him watching *her,* of all people. He had an odd smile on his face, as if pleased about something.

What was wrong with him? It was as though he *wanted* her to come to the worst possible conclusion.

Suddenly, Cathleen knew that was it. If she thought he was guilty, that would make it easier for him to walk away. And to justify having walked away the first time, too.

Ignoring the evidence, she spoke only what she knew in her heart to be true. "That isn't Dylan's. He doesn't even own a gun."

As soon as the words were out, Dylan's composure cracked. He hadn't expected her to stand up for him, not in the face of such a damning find.

"She's right," he said, as if he himself couldn't believe it. "That weapon doesn't belong to me. I've never seen it before."

"We'll see about that." Springer's confidence didn't waver in the slightest. "But you're coming with me for some questions."

"Wait, Thad." Cathleen put her hand on the sergeant's arm. He didn't seem to mind. She recalled the good-night kiss he'd given her after they'd gone to a movie. She'd touched his arm then, too, but that time it was to gently extricate herself from his embrace. "You're making a mistake."

"I'm afraid not. If you want to help Dylan, find him a good lawyer."

And then the men were gone, Dylan leaving without so much as a special smile or a meaningful look in her direction. Cathleen ran to the window, where she watched Springer open the back door of his cruiser. A low beam from the setting sun flashed against something metal. Cathleen almost groaned when she realized what had happened. Springer had put Dylan in handcuffs. Just like a common criminal.

DYLAN WAS SURPRISED at how much the handcuffs hurt. Sitting in the rear seat of the cruiser, his hands behind his back, he couldn't keep his balance. Each bump in the road, every curve and corner, forced him to shift his position and made the thick metal edges scrape his wristbones.

Of course, the physical discomfort was nothing compared with the humiliation. Springer was taking such obvious pleasure from this. Every time their glances collided the officer's eyes practically dripped triumph. And why not? The sergeant had won this round definitively, maybe won the whole fight.

Dylan had been coping with fear for so long. Worry about his mother, the future of his ranch and his chances with Cathleen had been a constant companion. But now, for the first time, he felt the lashes of a more elemental terror. He was going to be locked up and stripped of his personal freedom. Springer hadn't yet laid charges, but Dylan could tell by the fierce determination in the sergeant's eye that he would at the first opportunity.

Dylan was going down for *murder*. Never mind that he was innocent; it was happening. He would get a trial, of course, but would the truth be any less elusive than it was now? If that gun was indeed the murder weapon, he could be convicted. And of course the gun *would* turn out to be the murder weapon. Why else would someone have bothered to plant it there?

That was what puzzled Dylan. Most likely, Max had hidden the weapon under the mattress when he was in Cathleen's house that afternoon. But now, for the first time, Dylan considered the possibility that Max might actually be telling the truth about Rose, and that his alibi might be genuine.

So who else could have put the gun there? The answer was obvious. Thad Springer could easily have carried the murder weapon upstairs and pretended to find it under Dylan's mattress.

But was Thad so desperately in love with Cathleen that he would stoop to framing her boyfriend for murder just so she would be free? If he was, did that mean he'd killed Rose, as well? Dylan was willing to bet no one in the RCMP had thought to ask Springer for an alibi for that night.

At the detachment, Dylan had the opportunity to phone a lawyer. Springer removed the handcuffs and pushed him into a small room with a phone on the wall and a stool.

"Got someone in mind?" he asked.

"Not really." Dylan didn't know any criminal lawyers. Cathleen's sister Maureen might have some connections, but would she be willing to help him?

Springer gave him a list of Alberta lawyers, including some with Legal Aid, then left him to it. Dylan stared at the typed lines of names and numbers for a long time. His first instinct was to handle this on his own, arrange whatever legal representation he could find and take it from there.

But something Cathleen had said the other day was sticking in his head, something about being there for each other, him helping her and her helping him. He thought of the trust in her eyes as Springer led him out of her kitchen.

In this situation he knew what she'd want him to do. But was it the right thing?

Finally he picked up the phone and dialed a familiar number.

He got an answer on the fourth ring.

"Hello?" she said.

"Cathleen? I need your help."

KELLY HAD ALREADY POURED her a brandy and lit a fire in the study. Cathleen sank into the cushions on one end of the sofa and accepted the snifter thankfully.

"I take it that was Dylan," Kelly said.

Cathleen nodded. She was so relieved that he'd called. She'd expected him to retreat behind his macho do-it-yourself shield again. But this time he'd surprised her.

"He asked if I could call Maureen, and I had to admit I already had." Springer's vehicle had still been in full view when she'd picked up the phone. Maureen would have driven out for the weekend, but Holly was still upset from a recent session with a new grief counselor. What Maureen had been able to do, however, was give Cathleen several names of good criminal lawyers. Cathleen had passed the information on to Dylan. Along with her love.

"How are Dylan's spirits?" Kelly asked.

"Not bad. He's come up with two possibilities for who could have planted that gun under his bed."

If Kelly thought to herself that perhaps the gun hadn't been planted at all, she was wise enough not to say so. "I assume Max Strongman is one."

"Yes. He and James were here this afternoon while we were out. They let themselves in, supposedly to use the bathroom and to get some water."

"Well, that does sound suspicious," Kelly agreed. "Who else does Dylan think it could be?"

"This is the really crazy part." Truthfully, Cathleen didn't want to say anything. Kelly would think Dylan was a total basket case.

"Don't hold back on me."

"Fine." She took a long swallow of brandy for courage. "Dylan thinks Springer is so obsessed with me that he might have actually killed Rose and framed Dylan so that I would be free. Obviously Dylan is scraping the barrel with this one."

To her surprise, her sister didn't scoff. Instead, she curled up cross-legged on the opposite end of the sofa and rubbed the side of her neck thoughtfully.

"Springer has always been very good to me, but just about every time we have a conversation, he eventually turns the subject around to you. I used to find it kind of cute. These past few months though, it's been making me uncomfortable. Especially since Dylan came back.''

''Why didn't you say something to me?''

''I didn't think it was a big deal. But now...'' Kelly pulled the elastic from her hair and shook out her ponytail. ''Cathleen, I'm going to look into this. Maybe I can find out, discreetly, where Springer was that night. I know he was on duty, but that doesn't mean he couldn't have slipped away for a time without anyone noticing.''

''Please do.'' Although she didn't hold out much hope that this lead would get them any further than any of the others had, Cathleen was determined to turn over any stone that she could. Finally, Dylan had come to her for help, and more than anything, she didn't want to let him down.

DYLAN HAD BEEN TAKEN in for questioning on Saturday evening. Picturing him in a cold concrete holding cell, Cathleen couldn't sleep that night. All Sunday she waited for news, but heard nothing. Around two in the afternoon, Kelly returned from wherever she'd been all morning and suggested they make lunch.

''It's a wonder I have any hair left on my head,'' Cathleen confessed. ''This waiting around is driving me crazy. For the first time in my life, I wish

I had a cell phone. I don't want to go out in case I miss Dylan's call asking me to pick him up.''

''That's not likely to happen soon,'' Kelly said.

Cathleen had surmised as much, but having her fears confirmed sent her sagging into a chair. ''He'll be going crazy in there. Dylan hates to be cooped up in a house, let alone a cell.''

Kelly took over at the counter, buttering slices of bread. ''I talked to some of the guys this morning, including the front desk officer the night of the murder. I had to be circumspect, of course, but from what I can tell, no one can confidently vouch for Springer's whereabouts between nine and ten o'clock the evening Rose was killed.''

''So for now he stays on the list,'' Cathleen said. She forced herself up and to the fridge, where she found a package of sliced Black Forest ham.

''I'll take that.'' Kelly unwrapped the thin slices of meat and placed several on each sandwich, along with some lettuce and tomato.

Cathleen was cutting the sandwiches when the phone rang.

Thinking, hoping, it might be Dylan, she could have screamed when she heard James's voice on the end of the line.

''What do *you* want?'' She was beyond putting up polite pretenses.

''M-my father wanted me to call.''

Of course. James only ever did what his father

told him to. "Why? To gloat over the fact that Dylan's in custody?"

"Of course not. He just—that is, we were wondering if you'd considered our offer. We've had some papers drawn up. I could drop them by your place. Of course, you'll want to have a lawyer check them over, but it's all just as we said the other night."

Cathleen turned so Kelly could see her rolling her eyes. "You mean the night you broke in to my house so your father could hide the gun he used to kill Rose Strongman?"

"Wh-what? That's crazy!"

Even over the phone Cathleen could sense the insincerity of his protest. Did James know for sure what his father had done? Or was he, like them, only guessing?

"Not as crazy as the idea that the gun belonged to Dylan."

"How could we have slipped it under the mattress when we didn't even know which room was Dylan's?"

Oh, my God. Did he understand what he'd just said?

"Hang on a minute, James." She covered the mouthpiece and asked her sister a question. After Kelly's answer, she nodded. "I didn't think so."

Removing her hand, she spoke to James again. "You want to hear something interesting?"

"What?"

"You said the gun was found under Dylan's mattress, but the police haven't released any of this information to the public. The only people who knew where Springer found that gun were the RCMP, Dylan, Kelly and me." She waited for the meaning to sink in.

"Oh," she finally added, "plus the person who put it there."

CATHLEEN AND KELLY LEFT a note on the kitchen table for Poppy. Of necessity, it was long, explaining about the gun found under Dylan's mattress and how the RCMP had taken him into custody.

We're on the way to the detachment now, Cathleen wrote. *I'm positive James is the one who put the gun under Dylan's mattress. I just hope Springer believes me.*

Unwilling to wait for Dylan's lawyer to make the one-hour drive from Calgary, Cathleen headed for the detachment in her Jeep, with Kelly silent and anxious by her side. Kelly had the notebook she used at work in her hand, and was flipping past old entries.

In the clean, somewhat sterile reception room, Cathleen asked to speak to Springer. He came out almost immediately, crisply dressed and close shaven. Yet, there were signs of stress around his eyes and mouth. With a polite gesture, he ushered them both to his office.

"I just got off the phone with James Strongman," she explained as they walked, unable to wait to tell her story. She related the conversation as close to word for word as she could manage.

By the end, all three of them were sitting in Springer's office.

"So you see," she concluded, "either James or his father had to have put that gun there. How else could they have known where you found it?"

Thad frowned and tapped his fingers on his desk. "I'm afraid this doesn't prove as much as you think it does. Did anyone else hear this conversation?"

"Of course not! We were on the phone!" Good Lord, she didn't have the patience for this. "Look, get Dylan in here, would you? He should hear this, too."

"It won't make any difference," Thad warned, but he stuck his head out the open office door and asked someone to bring McLean to the bigger coffee room on the other side of the building.

As the three of them were walking there, someone burst through the main doors. A second later, Cathleen heard Poppy's voice.

"I need to speak to Sergeant Springer!"

Thad stopped short. "Jesus. What a circus." He detoured to the front desk and invited Poppy to join them. She entered dressed in colorful silk, her hair in curled disarray.

"Girls! I just read your note and came as quickly as I could. There's been a terrible mistake."

"Just a minute, please," Springer said, his voice tight and hard. "If we could sit down and discuss this calmly..."

The coffee room held a big rectangular table and plenty of chairs for everyone. No sooner had they settled than Dylan was admitted. Cathleen tried to catch his eye, but he wouldn't look at anyone except Springer. She could tell he was mortified by the undignified situation. At least he was still in his own clothes—admittedly a little rumpled—and not some awful prison uniform.

"Like I said, there's been a mistake. I always use hospital corners when I make the beds."

"Ma'am," Springer said a trifle condescendingly, "I haven't a clue what you're talking about."

Poppy sighed with frustration, then began again. "You found the gun under Dylan's mattress on Saturday evening, correct?"

"That's right," Springer confirmed.

"Well, Dylan couldn't have put it there because that morning, before I left for my weekend away, I made up the beds. And when I make a bed, I tuck the top sheet completely between the box spring and the mattress, with the corners neat, like this." Poppy took the scarf she'd been wearing under her jacket and spread it over a book on the table. Carefully, she demonstrated the procedure.

"See? In order to get these corners tucked in that way, it's necessary for me to lift the mattress a little. Enough that I'd surely see if a gun was under there."

Cathleen caught the smallest movement of Dylan's mouth. A slight curve of amusement.

Beside him, Springer frowned.

"Poppy is right," Cathleen added. "I stripped the beds that morning and noticed nothing unusual. Dylan was with me all day in Canmore, then he took my horse out for a ride before dinner. He had no chance to hide the gun after Poppy made the bed."

Springer pulled out his notebook. He flipped back a few pages. Read. Then frowned even more.

"But Max or James Strongman could have." Cathleen told the sergeant about the men's unscheduled visit and how they'd let themselves into her unlocked home. Then she told Dylan about James's phone call and how he'd known where Springer had found the gun.

"I don't see how he could've known that detail. Unless *he* stashed the gun there. Or watched his father do it." That James could've been his father's accomplice, she had no doubt. The poor man had never stepped out from his father's shadow. Besides, from a monetary perspective, he had as much to gain as Max did.

Springer rubbed a hand through his short brown hair. "I don't believe this…. The mayor?" For the first time he seemed to seriously consider the possibility, but then he shook his head. "No. It couldn't be Max. His alibi checked out."

"But what about James's alibi?" Kelly said. "Before my—my suspension, I did some investigating into this." She opened the notebook she'd been perusing in Cathleen's car.

"When originally questioned about that night, James claimed he was in Calgary, having dinner with several businessmen until about eleven at night. Given the hour's drive to Canmore, he couldn't possibly have shot his stepmother."

Springer nodded. "That's right."

"But," Kelly continued, "when we questioned the two men he had dinner with, they told us the meal was finished by eight-thirty. So he *could* have been back in time."

Springer swore. "Why wasn't I told of this?"

Kelly noted tentatively, "I gave you copies of the report."

"Shit! This makes us all look bad."

Springer asked to see Kelly's notebook. After reviewing the entries he heaved a sigh, then nodded in Dylan's direction, without looking at the man.

"Release him," he said unenthusiastically. "And bring James Strongman in for questioning."

CHAPTER SEVENTEEN

KELLY REPORTED BACK to Cathleen and Dylan the next evening. They were all three in the study and Dylan was savoring every moment of the peaceful night. For the first time in years, he felt fully and wonderfully free. No more shadows hung over him. His innocence was undisputed. Thanks to Poppy's hospital corners.

Yet life was far from rosy. Cathleen had moved his pack from her room back to his. The message was clear, but he had yet to broach the subject with her.

"So what happened when James was brought in for questioning?" Cathleen asked, making room for her sister on the sofa. "Did his daddy have all the answers written out for him on little index cards?"

"Maybe he did," Kelly said. "But James wasn't there to read them to us. According to the airline records, he took a flight to Puerto Vallarta, Mexico, about four hours after he got off the phone with you on Sunday night. We have no idea where he went from there. He didn't register at any of the hotels, nor did he rent a car. If he traveled by local bus, tracing him will be nearly impossible.''

"Bloody quick disappearing act,'' Dylan said.

"Thanks, no doubt, to his father. Do you think Max intends to hide him away like that forever?''

"He may have to,'' Kelly said. "We've been tracking down the murder weapon and we've found the guy who originally brought it over the border. He's identified James as the person he sold it to.''

"So you have a pretty solid case?'' Though as far as Dylan was concerned, it couldn't be too solid.

"We do. And Max is fully aware of it. He'll probably keep his son under wraps, if he can.''

"I wonder if we'll ever find out if Max was behind the murder, or whether James acted on his own.''

"One of my buddies let me go over the transcripts, Cathleen. My impression is that Max has been pretty shaken up by all this. I really don't think he had a clue what his son was up to. Although he may have figured it out soon afterward, and tried to help James pin the evidence on Dylan.''

Dylan respected Kelly's opinion, but to him things didn't add up. He just couldn't see James having planned and carried out this crime on his own. Plus there was the question of the Beckett homicide.

"I don't suppose the RCMP have tried to see if

James is implicated in Jilly's murder, as well,'' he said.

"We're considering the possibility," Kelly assured him. "But the evidence just isn't there one way or the other."

"I was in town today," Cathleen said, "and everyone I saw told me they were certain James must've killed Jilly Beckett, too. And why not? He'd been there that night."

How quickly the tides of public opinion could turn. In a weird way, Dylan almost felt sorry for James. For sure, he could never hate the man the way he despised Max. In too many ways, James himself had been a victim. Killing Rose could have been his twisted way of seeking his father's elusive approval.

"The phone has been ringing all day," Cathleen reported, "with people eager to assure us they never really believed Dylan was guilty."

Kelly laughed. "That figures."

Talk stalled for a few moments, as they ran out of new developments to discuss. Kelly glanced from her sister, to Dylan, then back again. Finally she asked the question everyone had been avoiding.

"What happens now?"

Dylan looked at Cathleen, but she kept her gaze downward. Since he'd been released from custody, she'd avoided his every attempt to speak to her intimately or to touch her. He just didn't get it.

When he was up to his eyeballs in muck, when it seemed that no one in the world was on his side, she'd been with him one hundred percent. Now that he finally had his reputation and good name to offer her, she wanted nothing to do with him.

"I've got a line on a foreman job," he told Kelly. "I'm moving in with Jake until the details are settled. He's back from Australia at the end of the week. I'm picking him up from the airport."

"I see." Kelly turned again to her sister, but Cathleen remained quiet.

He wished he knew what was going on in her head. When he'd needed help he'd asked her. He'd thought that was what she wanted, what she felt had been missing from their relationship. Apparently he'd read the situation wrong. Or maybe he'd just underestimated her stubbornness.

DYLAN WAS RELIEVED when, the next day, a couple visiting from Europe and their three small children dropped in for the night. The B and B was back in business. Cathleen settled her guests in the Valley-view Room, which had a double bed, a set of bunks and, of course, a view down the Bow Valley.

Noise, laughter and heart-shaped pancakes ruled at the breakfast table the next morning. By this point, Dylan was desperate for time alone with Cathleen, especially since this was his last night at the B and B.

After the family checked out—with promises to return following their visit to Jasper—he persuaded Cathleen to drive into Canmore with him and grab an espresso at the Grazing Grounds.

Inside the funky café, he'd hoped to find a quiet table for two, but the place was packed. Beth Gibson was in line in front of them. He still wasn't sure what to make of the woman. She seemed to have similarly ambivalent feelings about him. After a quick double take, she made a visible effort of will and stepped forward to offer her hand.

"I must apologize, Dylan. I jumped to conclusions and made some pretty deplorable accusations."

"Not to worry. You weren't the only one." Frankly, the opinions of others had never concerned him that much. It was their effect on Cathleen he'd worried about.

At any rate, he didn't intend to carry a grudge against anyone who had shunned him earlier. How could he? Even Cathleen's sisters had doubted his innocence, although they'd both apologized profusely these past few days.

"You take care now." Beth picked up the two lattes she'd ordered and returned to the table where her husband waited with toasted bagels and the local paper. Dylan watched as her spouse helped Beth settle in her seat, before passing her one of the bagels. Amicably they divided the paper into sections, sharing a quick kiss before dipping into the morning's news.

They appeared so comfortable together, and affectionate, that Dylan hoped he and Cathleen had been way off base in their speculation of an illicit affair between Beth and Max.

"Here's your coffee." Cathleen had ordered him the largest size—the sweetheart.

"Thanks, darlin'." He scooped some change from his pocket and set it on the counter, then touched his fingers to her elbow. "How about we find someplace quiet to enjoy these."

"Such as?"

"The bridge?"

"Oh!" She sounded unsure, but she fell into stride beside him without complaint.

Brilliant sunshine blended with the cool air flowing off the Rockies. Ahead, looking as if they'd been sculpted out of the sky, were the peaks of familiar mountains. Surrounding trees had lost all but the most stalwart of leaves.

"This is the spot, isn't it?" Dylan leaned over the railing and checked out the meandering creek below.

"Where you asked me to marry you?" Cathleen sipped her coffee, then answered her own question. "I believe it is, yes."

A shiver crawled down his spine. He had an awful feeling this wasn't going to go well. Still, he had to do it. The longer he delayed, the crazier it made him.

There was no doubt he'd scored a victory this week—being released from that damn holding cell and vindicated in the eyes of friends and family—but it meant squat if Cathleen wasn't part of his future.

Dylan had tried to think up something fancy and poetic to say at this moment. In the end, he could find only three words, the same three he'd used the first time.

"Marry me, Cathleen?"

Four years ago, his question had been met with a no-holds-barred hug, tears, laughter and, best of all, an emphatic *yes*. Today, his proposal fell into silence, with Cathleen averting her head and leaving him totally in the dark about her feelings.

Dylan squeezed the wooden railing and cursed himself silently. Maybe if he'd given her a few more weeks…

Gathering his courage, he wrapped one arm around her waist and used the other to tilt her face toward him. Gently he kissed her cheek, her chin, the bridge of her nose.

"It's not going to fly this time, huh?"

She broke from his arms and leaned against the railing. In profile, he saw her bottom lip tremble as she gazed at the mountains. "I can't do this again, Dylan. I won't."

His heart hung like a deadweight in his chest. "What do you mean?"

"I love you, I'm not pretending I don't. But I've also made it clear, ever since you came back, that I wasn't going through all that again."

"I was a horse's ass to leave you."

Her mouth twitched. Was it a smile?

"At least you've finally got your apology right," she said.

"Hey, I'm learning." In fact, he'd learned a lot, most of it in these past three weeks. The first time he'd proposed to Cathleen all he'd cared about was how much he loved her and wanted to be with her. On some level he'd probably modeled his expectations on his own parents' marriage. Which had been happy enough for them, but wouldn't fit him or Cathleen worth a damn.

This time he'd actually done some thinking about the kind of partnership they *would* make together. He'd realized that the very characteristics that differentiated her from Rose were part of what attracted him so much to Cathleen.

Not that he hadn't loved his mother. But he'd always enjoyed a good challenge. And Cathleen was that, all right.

"I don't expect you to be the kind of wife my mother was—Lord, it's the last thing I'd want. I love you for your strength, your independence, your spirit."

He'd felt confident that this time he was finally on the right track. But Cathleen only seemed to become sadder.

"You're saying all the right things, Dylan. But I just can't wipe the slate clean. And I can't help asking myself if you truly believe what you're saying, or if you're just saying the things you think I want to hear."

"But after all we've been through... Why did you stand by me if you didn't want to be with me?"

"It's way more complicated than what I *want*. It's a question of doing the right thing, the *smart* thing. Dylan, I knew you were innocent, so of course I did everything I could to help prove that you were. But that doesn't mean I can marry you."

"I won't leave you again, Cathleen. I promise." He'd never been more sincere in his life. But she wouldn't even look at him as she bent to pick up something from the ground. It was a leaf from a nearby poplar, golden and perfect. With care, she let it flutter from her fingers to the water below. He watched it land, then slowly float away.

"I'll bet my father said something similar to my mother each time he came back to her. You promised before, Dylan. That's what that ring you gave me was all about. It said your future was mine, that we would always be together. But you left. You broke your word to me."

He couldn't think of anything to say. There was

no defense. He'd hoped that she would forgive what he'd done, that she would understand he'd felt he had no choice.

But now she placed her hand on his arm, and he stared at it with the sense of seeing something precious and familiar that was suddenly not what he'd thought it to be.

"So this is really it?" he said finally.

"Yes, Dylan. It is."

And just like that he lost her.

ABOUT A MONTH HAD GONE BY since Cathleen had last paid the bills and balanced her checking account. As usual, she put off the task until two days before the due date on her VISA statement. Poppy was in bed. Cathleen had just finished the dishes.

Kelly was out on a late-night drive, God knows where. Cathleen worried about her. As far as she could tell, the counseling sessions weren't doing much good. And just this evening Kelly had announced that she planned to move back to her basement apartment on the weekend.

Cathleen didn't think she was ready to be on her own. But how could she stop her?

Kip followed her from the kitchen down the hall to the study. The room was dark and chilly. Cathleen switched on the desk lamp, then laid a fire. Once heat was seeping into the room, Crystal emerged from one of her hiding places and curled up on the rug, which had once been Kip's spot.

Displaced, Kip circled the kitty for a few moments before finally giving in and lying next to her.

Cathleen poured herself a brandy and settled at the desk. The pile of unopened mail was daunting. She hadn't looked at any of it in almost two weeks.

And she didn't particularly want to deal with it now.

"Oh, damn it anyway..." Her head sank to the desk, cushioned in her arms. Briefly she closed her lids over eyes that burned from the tears that she would not shed. Sleep was a seductive suitor these days, calling to her at all hours but ensnaring her for only the briefest snatches of time. An hour or two might pass, then she would awake with a start, as if a shot of adrenaline had been injected into her bloodstream.

At each rousing, she felt the same chilling panic. *Did I do the right thing? Should I have accepted Dylan's proposal?*

Even now, about to drift off in a nap, she jerked up at the thought.

She could call him this minute and tell him she'd made a mistake. In half an hour they could be in each other's arms.

It was what she wanted, what she craved. So why not do it? Even her sisters and Poppy had prodded her with gentle hints. She and Dylan loved each other. It ought to be enough.

Yet it hadn't been for Dylan. He'd walked away two years ago because he'd needed more, or he'd thought she needed more. Either way, the outcome was the same.

The man she loved most was the person who'd wounded her the deepest. Was she petty not to just forgive him and put the past behind her? But what good had that approach done her mother? She'd given their father three chances and he'd still left.

Her mother had raised her not to put up with that kind of behavior from a man. Her mother had raised her to have pride and respect for herself.

Cathleen reached for her brandy, took a sip, then grabbed the pile of letters. As she leafed through them, one envelope stood out. The paper was thicker, creamier, and the envelope itself was larger than the standard-size ones her bills usually came in.

She turned it over, but there was no return address. Her name and address were typed in a flowing script.

With the end of her thumbnail, she slit it open. Onto her desk fluttered a single sheet of paper, with a violet embossed in the top right corner:

Dylan Brice McLean
requests the honor of your presence

at his marriage to
Cathleen Redmond Shannon
on Saturday, the thirteenth of October
at six o'clock in the evening
at Ralph Connor United Church
Canmore, Alberta

It had to be a joke. Cathleen read the invitation over several more times, her heart speeding up with each reading.

If it was a joke, it was a bloody poor one. Who would be so cruel? Not her sisters. Surely not Dylan.

Cathleen reached once more for her brandy. The sweet orange liquid glided warmly down her throat, calming the jitters in the pit of her stomach. Maybe it wasn't a joke. Maybe Dylan had planned a wedding and sent out invitations on his own.

She felt a moment's joy at the daring of it, the romance... Then anger set in. How could he be so sure of her? They hadn't spoken since his proposal on the bridge in town. Only an arrogant fool would print up invitations to a wedding that the bride had turned down.

With a jerk, she pushed herself up from the desk. Thoughts flashed in her head like bolts of lightning. Viewed with a little perspective, this latest maneuver was just like Dylan. He was always so sure of himself, so arrogant, so...so...Dylan-like!

Cathleen turned out her desk lamp. Her coat and car keys were by the back door. She didn't care that it was past midnight. Dylan owed her some answers, and she was going to get them. Now.

THE LIGHTS WERE OUT at Jake Hartman's town house. Jake's Expedition and Dylan's Ford were parked single file in the drive.

Cathleen slammed on her brakes, blocking off the end of the driveway with her Jeep. She got out of the vehicle, banging the door. Clouds obscured the moon and stars on this cold night in early October, but attractive light poles, straight from Dickens's London, illuminated the brick path that led to the front door.

Cathleen ignored that route. She was willing to guess the master suites in this development all faced south, toward the mountains and the creek. Which meant that the guest bedroom windows would be in front, over the garages.

Her boots slid on the frost-slicked grass as she walked toward a graveled path where she could pick up a few pebbles. She warmed them in her palm while she took stock of her target. The window seemed to be open. If she was lucky…

She let loose with a volley and her aim was true. Some of the gravel ended up in the room. The rest rattled satisfactorily against the upper half of the glass pane. She waited a few minutes, then in a loud whisper called, "Dylan!"

A lamp switched on, and a naked man appeared at the window, visible from mid-chest up. "What in the world...?"

She tossed another handful of gravel, smiling as he stepped back in a hurry.

"Ow!" He cursed a few times, sank out of sight, then reappeared with a pillow clutched in front of him. "That you, Cathleen?"

"Get down here," she said as loud as she dared. "I want to talk to you."

A few moments passed. Dylan picked up something from the floor and stepped into it. Probably his jeans.

Finger-combing his hair, he leaned out the window. "Come inside. I'll pour us a drink."

He looked disheveled and disoriented, like someone who'd been soundly asleep. She resented that fact as much as anything. She hadn't had a decent night's sleep in forever.

"I don't want a drink. I just want to talk. Meet me at my Jeep." She stalked from the house back to her vehicle.

It took less than a minute for Dylan to emerge from the front door. Damn him to hell, with his sleep-tousled hair and bare chest, jeans zipped but the top button unfastened, he was impossibly sexy.

"Well, this is an unexpected pleasure, darlin'."

His grin was pure masculine charm and she wanted to kick him in the shin.

"Don't give me any of your bullshit, Dylan. I want to know what the hell this—thing!—was doing in my mail." She took the invitation and slammed it into his chest.

He was quick, grabbing the piece of paper and her hand, before she had a chance to pull away.

"Didn't you like the stationery? I thought the violet was just your style."

She had loved that violet. The violet was perfect. That he'd known her well enough to pick it made the whole escapade so much more intolerable.

"You've pulled some capers in the past, Dylan. But don't you think this is stooping rather low? A wedding just doesn't make a good subject for a practical joke."

"That invitation is dead serious. As I am."

He tugged on her arm, drawing her right to his chest. His bare, muscular chest, which she had kissed and caressed and laid her head on for comfort a thousand times before.

Lord, she was *melting,* like a chocolate left out in the sun.

She watched the kiss coming as if in time-lapse photography, each second drawn out to an eternity of frustrated longing. By the time their lips met, it was impossible to say who had wanted it more.

She opened her mouth to the demands of his

tongue, and the sweet aftertaste of brandy that he, too, must have drunk that evening. She placed her hands on either side of his face, as he pressed her back to the Jeep, his arms a cushion against the cold, hard metal.

"Dylan..." If it was possible for a man and a woman to become one from just a single kiss, then it was happening. She felt as if her very essence was being sucked out from within her. And greedily, she took as much as she was giving.

When his mouth moved impatiently to her neck, she dropped her head back against the Jeep and twined one leg around the back of his knees, tilting her pelvis to meet his.

Dylan silenced her moans with yet another kiss, this one fractionally more gentle. Whether it was his deliberate change in the tempo of their lovemaking or merely the passage of time that allowed a return of her sanity, Cathleen remembered what she was doing there in the first place.

"I said," she repeated, "that I wouldn't marry you."

Wrapped in Dylan's arms, her heart still pounding passionately and the taste of him vivid in her mouth, she knew her words sounded preposterous. She pushed him away.

He sighed, then reached out to settle a wayward strand of her hair. "You also said you loved me. And it's true, isn't it?"

"Of course." She stared down at her everyday brown riding boots. Did he think she could kiss him like that if it wasn't?

"Then I don't see why you wouldn't marry me."

"I can't *trust* you, you damn idiot. That's why!"

"Come on, Cathleen. You can't expect me to buy that." He crossed his arms over his chest and shook his head.

"I travel all the way from Nevada just to see you and work like the devil to clear my name. I ask you to marry me, even go to the trouble of planning the whole wedding so all you have to do is get dressed and walk down the aisle. And you think, after all that, there's even the slightest chance that *I* won't show up?"

Cathleen dug her heels into the gravel on the side of the road. "That's not the point. Marriage is about partnership and you—"

"Don't give me that bull, Cathleen. I'm willing to be your partner and you know it. I can't believe you'd let your pride stand in the way of our future."

Cathleen jerked away from him. "You think this is about my *pride?*"

"Of course it is. That's why I organized the wedding like this. If you want, you can stand me up on October 13. That'll make us even."

Her head spun with the outrageousness of it all.

"You mean you planned this wedding, *expecting* I wouldn't attend?"

"Well, it would be nice if you did. But I won't blame you if you don't."

She wished it wasn't dark, so she could read his expression. This plan was just too crazy for him to be serious. "And what if I don't? What then?"

"Then we'll be even. And we can plan a third wedding," he said. "And that time, we'll both show up."

There had to be something fishy going on here. "How many people did you invite?" Probably only a handful. Or nobody. Chances were he hadn't even booked the church or spoken to the minister....

"Eighty-five. Counting you. I gave Poppy and Kelly their invitations when I saw them in town. Ask them."

He sounded so serious.... "October 13 is less than two weeks away!"

"Well, I didn't figure you'd need much time, since you already have a dress."

"I told you I threw that out."

"Uh-huh."

"Forget it, Dylan." She pulled her keys from her jacket pocket and walked round to the driver's side of the Jeep. "An interesting scheme, I'll give you that. But it isn't going to work."

He faced her with a final smile. "Till October

13, Cathleen. I can hardly wait. You've always looked spectacular in white.''

"IT ISN'T JUST PRIDE," Cathleen repeated to her dog later that night. It was three in the morning and she was sitting up in bed. Cool air and moonlight spilled in through her open window. A mug of stone-cold chamomile tea sat on her bedside table. The brandy glass next to it was empty.

"It's a question of principle. Of not letting anyone take advantage of you," she elaborated.

Kip tilted his head to one side. Of course it was easy for a dog. Good people scratched you behind the ears and gave you treats from the table. Dylan had won Kip over long ago. That didn't mean she should marry him, though.

"Then what does it mean?" she wondered aloud. "It's *not* just a question of pride."

Kip yawned, turned around once, then settled into his corduroy bed. He'd given up on her. Something Crystal had done long ago. The white feline was sleeping curled up on Dylan's—no, not Dylan's—the *extra* pillow by her side.

Cathleen slid a little lower under the covers and let her head fall back on her own pillow. She was ready to give up on herself, too. Besides, she was tired. Finally. She closed her eyes and let out a sigh.

It was the principle of the thing. Love isn't always enough.... The words buzzed in her head, but she had to let them go. She was so exhausted her bones actually ached. She flung out one arm and a second later, felt Kip lick her hand.

"That's nice," she said sleepily, liking the fact that she wasn't alone. Her companions were just a cat and a dog, true, but at least she wasn't alone.

She rolled onto her side. Sleep hovered so tantalizingly close she could feel it settling over her like an early-morning fog. What had she been thinking? Oh yes, the violet.

It was a very nice touch.

CHAPTER EIGHTEEN

DYLAN WAS WEARING A TUX for the first time in his life. Not just the jacket and pants, with that ribbon of silk running down the sides of his legs, but the whole "frou-fra": white shirt with cuff links and funny little covers for all the buttons, a ridiculous little black tie and matching sashlike thing for around his waist.

He looked like a fool. Not because of his clothes, but because it was now quarter past six, and she wasn't here.

The church was full. Every person he'd invited to this wedding had come—except for one. He'd mentally crossed names off the list he'd compiled with Jake's and Kelly's help, and as far as he could determine, Thad Springer was the only invited guest who hadn't shown up.

Except for the bride.

His friends from his ranching days were present, a few buddies from school, all of Cathleen's family...

Beside him, looking far too amused than was wise, stood his cousin Jake. Then there was that big gaping hole where the bride was supposed to be, and finally Kelly. The youngest Shannon sister was stunning in her off-the-shoulder, blue silk dress, but Jake didn't seem to notice. He kept glancing at the eldest sister, Maureen, perched nervously in the front pew with her eleven-year-old daughter, Holly.

Come on, Cathleen! Dylan tried to will her to the church through the power of positive thinking. He didn't care what she wore—jeans and her riding boots would be fine. All he wanted was for her to be there, to put her hand in his, to step up in front of the minister with him.

But there was no sign of her.

He pulled at the tie that choked his throat—as if he wasn't suffering enough, already—and shuffled his feet. For the first time, he grasped what it must have been like for Cathleen when he'd stood her up two years ago. True, he hadn't left her standing at the church. But it must've been mortifying for her to face her family and friends in the weeks after the scheduled event, knowing how much they'd be pitying her....

Dylan felt a bead of moisture trickle down the side of his forehead as he considered how they must be pitying him now.

It was twenty past six—he'd surreptitiously looked at his watch. Glancing to his left, he noticed Jake's grin broaden. His cousin winked, then straightened his shoulders. Dylan shifted his weight from his toes to his heels.

"What time did you say her appointment at the hairdresser's was?" he whispered loudly to Kelly.

A few giggles came from the pews, but Kelly just rolled her eyes and shook her head. *I warned you this wasn't such a great idea,* she seemed to be saying to him.

He was forced to agree. Apparently, he was being stood up. He would take the humiliation with as much grace as he could muster. Ten more minutes, and the show would be over. Should he still host the dinner he'd booked at the Canmore Hotel? Or just tell everyone to go home?

Then suddenly the organist—who'd ceased playing on a signal from Dylan about ten minutes ago—started that Bach number about joy again. The sound swelled, filling the empty space above them with the uplifting melody. All heads swiveled to the back of the church. Dylan shifted onto his toes, craning his neck, peering hopefully for a sign....

But no one was there.

A collective sigh fell. Then the organist hit the next chord, and suddenly she appeared.

Cathleen, in white, wearing a veil and holding flowers he'd ordered delivered to her house.

She'd come! She'd come!

A bride could not have looked more enchanting than she did. He could feel the spell settling over him as she floated nearer. Now he could see her features under that veil…her eyes were fixed on him, only him, and she was smiling.

Dylan felt a tear roll down his cheek. He was so happy, so unbelievably happy, that he wanted to rush toward her and gather her in his arms. But this was her moment, her chance to shine.

He noticed the dress—its fine-textured silk; its neckline, with its alluring hint of cleavage. Was it the same one she'd planned to wear two years ago?

She was close enough now that he could hold out his hand. As she reached for his fingers, he saw a flash of brilliant color, and realized she was wearing his ring.

So much for that ad in the *Leader*. She'd saved it after all. She'd waited two years and never stopped loving him. The way he'd never stopped loving her.

He entwined his fingers with hers, gripping her extra tight, in case last-minute nerves had her trying to run away from him.

But she didn't look as though she wanted to go anywhere. Even with the layer of gauze shielding them, he could see that her eyes were gleaming with happy tears, that her smile was warm and loving.

"Ready?" he asked her.

She nodded. "Let's do it, cowboy." With one hand she bunched up the fabric on her dress so they could step toward the minister together. The resulting flash of color had Dylan grinning in earnest.

She'd worn her red cowboy boots. Damn, but they were going to have one hell of a wedding night!

The Shannon Sisters

A Trilogy by C.J. Carmichael
The stories of three sisters from Alberta whose lives and loves are as rocky—and grand—as the mountains they grew up in.

A Second-Chance Proposal
A murder, a bride-to-be left at the altar, a reunion. Is Cathleen Shannon willing to take a second chance on the man involved in these?

A Convenient Proposal
Kelly Shannon feels guilty about what she's done, and Mick Mizzoni feels that he's his brother's keeper—a volatile situation, but maybe one with a convenient way out!

A Lasting Proposal
Maureen Shannon doesn't want risks in her life anymore. Not after everything she's lived through. But Jake Hartman might be proposing a sure thing....

On sale starting February 2002

Available wherever Harlequin books are sold.

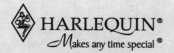

This Mother's Day Give Your Mom A Royal Treat

Win a fabulous one-week vacation in Puerto Rico for you and your mother at the luxurious Inter-Continental San Juan Resort & Casino. The prize includes round trip airfare for two, breakfast daily and a mother and daughter day of beauty at the beachfront hotel's spa.

INTER·CONTINENTAL
San Juan
RESORT & CASINO

Here's all you have to do:

Tell us in 100 words or less how your mother helped with the romance in your life. It may be a story about your engagement, wedding or those boyfriends when you were a teenager or any other romantic advice from your mother. The entry will be judged based on its originality, emotionally compelling nature and sincerity. See official rules on following page.

Send your entry to:

Mother's Day Contest

In Canada	**In U.S.A.**
P.O. Box 637	P.O. Box 9076
Fort Erie, Ontario	3010 Walden Ave.
L2A 5X3	Buffalo, NY
	14269-9076

Or enter online at www.eHarlequin.com

PRROY